In Between Pastures

Nora Kelly, Volume 2

Sequoyah Branham

Published by Sequoyah Branham, 2024.

This is a work of fiction. Similarities to real people, places, or events are entirely coincidental.

IN BETWEEN PASTURES

First edition. October 24, 2024.

Copyright © 2024 Sequoyah Branham.

ISBN: 979-8988190035

Written by Sequoyah Branham.

For the friends who won't let me do life alone.

Madeline, Juliet, Alabama, and Amanda thank you for being the support I sometimes don't know I need!

In Between Pastures

By Sequoyah Branham

Chapter 1

"Which one of these jugs is yours?" Uncle Ian's voice carries from the end of his old Chevy ranch pickup.

My long braid falls over my shoulder as I strain to get the fence stretcher to tighten the barbed wire one more notch. "What's that?" I wipe my palms on the butt of my jeans and walk over to him.

Ian points to our matching stainless steel half gallon water jugs sitting on the pickup bed. He flashes his classic half-smirk. "Do you remember where you set your water?"

I chuckle. "Not really." I turn one upside down. The sun has heated the steel almost too hot to hold. "This one still has the sticker on the bottom, so I think it's mine." I set it back on the tailgate with a clang.

He goes to the driver's door and rummages in the pocket. Reappearing with a screwdriver, he turns his jug on its side and starts chiseling. "There. Now I'll know." He holds it up to show a janky 'IK' on the side for Ian Kelly.

He always has a fix for everything.

I screw the lid back on mine and hold it out. "You want to do mine too?"

With a chuckle he takes it, but he does more than just an 'N'. He spells Nora all the way out. "Now no one else can claim it."

I return his grin as I take the lid off. "Thank you." It takes several good swallows before the lukewarm water has done much in cutting the sticky saliva from my mouth. I screw the lid back on and squint down the line of posts that drop off into the draw and out the other side. "Do you think we'll have this all patched up before your new cows get here?" He leased this little spread with them in mind.

I unroll a span of stay wire and clip it off from the fifty pound roll on his pickup bed. At Ian's silence, I glance over at him. Face twisted up in a grimace and hand on his chest, he swallows hard with a shake of his head.

That's weird.

He notices me watching him and waves a hand dismissively in the air. "Been having a lot of indigestion lately." Blinking, he clears his throat. Eyes down the fence, he nods. "I think we'll have it patched. The corner isn't that far across there."

I take another big drink of water then pick up my pliers. "I guess we better get at it then." With a fence that hasn't been maintained in twenty years, we sure have our work cut out for us.

Ian hands me one end of the fence stretcher. I have to readjust twice before I get it to the part of my hand that has callouses two inches thick. That thing is *hot*.

Squatting down to reach the bottom wire, I get the stretcher situated. "What did you get into yesterday afternoon?"

His end of the wire already in the stretcher, he starts ratcheting them toward one another. "I said to heck with this heat and had me an afternoon nap."

My eyebrows nearly touch each other in the middle of my forehead. Ian isn't a nap kind of guy. We've been going at it hard though—fixing fences, putting in a new water line. Shoot, I'd be up for a nap if I didn't have horse club practices and water leaks springing up like weeds. "That sounds nice." But something about him taking a nap doesn't sit right.

"It was." He drags the roll of barbed wire toward him and snips off a piece.

Darn. I could have gotten that for him, if I had been paying attention.

"What's it looking like down the fence? Are we going to rebuild another quarter mile?" I try to make my voice light as I step off down the fence. *Please tell me the fence even exists down here.*

The wire along the county road almost didn't exist. We spent last week fixing that little issue. I step over a prickly pear, veer around a head-high bushy mesquite, and put on the brakes. *Lovely. Looks like we'll be doing about the same over here.*

"Fence that good, huh?" The sarcasm in Ian's voice puts a little pep back in my step.

I step around the bushy mesquite and give him a baby grin. "The top two wires are broke. Who knows when there stopped being a fourth wire on the bottom."

He disappears from view. I gingerly reach for the closest end of the top wire that lays nestled in tubosa grass and prickly pear. I'll have enough little brown thorns in my hand without shoving it in the middle of prickly pear.

When I pull, it doesn't budge. I adjust my grip and jerk. A couple of prickly pear pads fall loose from the rest of the plants.

There we go.

I drape that end of the wire back on this side of the fence. Past a couple of t-posts, I find the other piece of the same wire and pull it loose. Ian's unearthed the bottom strand and has moved on to stretching the top one.

The day I finally outwork this man, I won't even enjoy it. He'll be one of those legends that's flanking calves at eighty. Oh well, I'll just uncover this end of the bottom one and see how big of a gap we'll have to fill in.

Ian twists the splice into place then hands me the extra set of pliers. "How's it been with those kiddos and their ponies?"

My lips spread so wide my ears move. Ian's been almost as invested in these kids as I have since I started coaching them. "Going pretty good. April's about to the point where she's going to start running the legs off that poor gray horse. Jake, he's almost got his mom talked into letting him enter in the next sorting the horse club has."

Ian's face lights up like a porch light. I smile too. Did he and Denise do all these things with Kayla when she was a little girl? We never talk about my late cousin much. Maybe in time, but a couple years is still pretty fresh.

"One of these days I'll get you and James talked into sorting with me." I shake my head and snip off a good chunk of rusted wire. "If the two of you team up I'll be toast."

He laughs. "How's James doing these days?"

I start splicing the bottom wire in with a new piece. "I haven't talked to him a whole lot. I keep pestering him to come sort with us so we can catch up, but I guess Wade is keeping him tied up."

He hands me the fence stretcher. *It'd be nice if we had two of these.* Maybe I'll dig around and find mine tonight.

"Ole Wade. Have you seen the old boss since you left?"

Each end of the wire in the stretcher, I ratchet it a couple of notches. "Saw him at the post office a couple months after Clay's cattle had come in. Seems like he'll be able to hang onto the rest of the cattle and keep James on."

"Good, good." He looks around and wipes the sweat from underneath his hat. "It'll rain one of these days."

"Every day is one day closer." I twist wire together with the pliers. The words don't come out half as cheerful as I want them to. When a sigh comes from behind me, my heart aches a little. In this business we're all always waiting on a rain.

My hands are full of tools, moving them down the fence to the next spot, when my phone vibrates from my hip pocket. It rings a few times while I shuffle the last few yards. Dropping the tools in a heap, I pull out my phone and slide the green circle across the screen. "Hello."

Clay Hatfield's business voice greets me. "Hi Nora, how's it going?"

I wipe sweat off my top lip and want to make a smart remark, but just mutter, "Not too bad."

As usual, my boss gets straight to the reason he called. "When you caked the bulls the other day, did you have all of them?"

A little weighted ball settles in my gut. *Here we go again.* "I was short one. He's pretty old and doesn't fight. He's been hanging back across that big wash, so the others will leave him be."

He hums a noise, and I can nearly see his wheels grinding.

Squatting in the shade of the mesquite, I pick up a pair of pliers and turn them over in my hand. *He's fine, I promise.*

Clay hums in thought. "Is there any way to cross that wash?"

It's not fit for man or beast to do, but it's possible. "Yes, sir." I glance up the fence at Ian still working away.

"I'd really like to know they're there. Warby's had a couple cases of cattle theft over his desk the last few weeks."

My eyes almost roll too far back in my head. *Nobody stole an old worn-out Hereford bull.* "Yes sir, I'll get over there first thing in the morning and look for him."

"Thanks Nora. Let me know when you find him."

I get out another 'yes sir' and then the line goes dead. Letting out an airy chuckle, I shake my head. "Ever get scared that your worn-out bull got stolen?"

Ian laughs. "Can't rightly say I've considered that option. Layed down and died maybe."

I shake my head again. "I guess I'll be beating the bushes in the morning."

"If you need to take off, I can plod along here."

Picking up a piece of wire, I shrug his suggestion off. "They're already bushed up for the afternoon. Besides, we've got to get to the corner before it gets to brushing up time for us."

***

On the drive to town, sweat soaks the back of my shirt just from leaning up against the seat. It wasn't quite that damp this morning patching fence with Ian. *And it's only May.*

I pull up a couple yards away from the arena gate and cut the engine. Looking across the recently plowed dirt, I contemplate what kind of battle I want to fight today. The "I don't want to ride fast" battle or the "my horse doesn't like the flag" battle. All three of the horse club kids I coach have come a long way, but the flag race is definitely their weakest event.

I sigh. *They'll never get better at flags if we don't tackle them.*

While I scrape enough dirt into three buckets for them to hold a flag, parents help kids get mounted. Buckets on top of barrels and kids horseback, I wave the youngsters over.

They chatter about what went on at school and who got more recess time. I smile. Kids are something else.

"Alright." I clap my hands, and their heads swivel so they're looking at me. "Let's work on flag races today."

A couple groans mix with the one cheer. Kaelee is the only one impressed with that idea. I point each kid to a different colored bucket and pull little velvet flags from my back pocket. "First, ride by and stick the flag in the bucket. Make sure it's standing up right."

"Mickey doesn't like to get close to the barrels," Trace says.

"That's why we're practicing it." I hold out a green flag to the little seven year old boy.

April raises her hand. "Um, M-miss Nora..." Her voice gets weaker with every syllable.

I nod. "It's alright. Just try it at a walk and you can work up from there." Some days she and Charlie are full of ambition. Other days he's a pill and sucks her confidence.

I hand the girls each a flag and watch them trot away from me. Stepping back to the fence, I prop one foot up against it.

Kaelee's dad walks up to the fence a couple feet down from me and leans his forearms on it from the opposite side. "I'm glad they listen to you."

I laugh. "Do they though?" *Sometimes I wonder.*

"A lot better than they listen to their parents." He chuckles.

April and Charlie walk halfway to the barrel before she kicks him up to a trot. I smile. *That's my girl.* She gets Charlie to side step over close enough for her to plant the flag in the bucket. Loping back toward me, her face sports a smile that lights up her whole little eight-year-old body. I clap and give her a thumbs up.

Busy watching April, I'm a little slow to realize the struggle Trace is having with Mickey. The little horse gets almost close enough to the barrel, but the moment Trace leans over Mickey is side stepping away. Jumping off the fence, I start across the arena to the pair.

"Mickey! Stop it." Trace pulls the rein around to his hip and the horse circles away from the barrel.

"Hold on. Just make him stand by the barrel for a second." The deep arena dirt locks my boots in it with each step, taking twice as long for me to cover the distance.

The roan pony chews on the bit, nose pointed towards the gate they came in. Trace's little fingers are clamped around the reins, but he's not pulling on the horse's mouth.

He's learned the most important thing anyway.

I put one hand on the rein and the other on the swell of the little saddle. One look at Trace's face and I'm pretty sure we're one failed attempt from a come-apart.

"Good job staying with him." The praise brings no reaction from the kid. I can understand that. "Let's try again and I'll stay on his off side so he can't turn out. Okay?"

A nod is all the response I get.

"Take up on your inside rein just a little bit. That keeps his head turned in and makes it harder for him to go away from the barrel." I give Trace a nod to go ahead and then pierce the pony with a stare.

Quit being such a turd.

I end up poking Mickey in the ribs with my thumb a couple times so he stands up, but Trace gets the flag in the bucket. He high fives me with an undercover grin.

"Why don't you try one more time before we move on?"

The little boy nods and takes his pony in a big circle before coming back next to the barrel. It still takes some work, but he gets it done. I give him a big thumbs up. *They're getting there.*

"Girls, come back in here and we'll start our game." I get them lined up to play horseback tag and then perch myself on the fence. If I stand much longer my legs might give out. They're toast from the all the squatting and walking we've been doing on that fence.

Thank goodness Ian's cattle will be in soon. Then things will slow down a bit.

Chapter 2

Spurs jingling in the still morning air, I step in the saddle house and study my bridles. I reach for Cante's hackamore and head into my geldings' pen. Their silhouettes come to attention at the screech of the gate latch. Dune throws his head in the air and trots to the other corner.

Troublesome middle child.

I eye Cante, the youngster of the bunch, and ease toward him. He snorts as I draw a rein around his neck. "You're fine," I mumble and slide the bosal over his nose.

Out of the pen and in front of the saddle house, Cante lets out a big breath and cocks a hind leg. "Good boy. See, you *can* relax."

In a few short minutes, the big sorrel is saddled, and my legs are clad in leather leggins. I load him in the trailer and head off toward the now oranging eastern sky.

The caliche dust hangs in the sky as I unload Cante. He's finally settling down enough to be a pretty relaxing ride to wander around the country on. But not so relaxed that he doesn't keep one ear cocked back at me as I jump, catch the stirrup with the toe of my boot, and swing into the saddle. I lift my rope out from under my right leg and give his sorrel neck a pat.

"Alright bud, let's find us a bull."

He parts the greasewood bushes with his long strides, and in a moment we're looking off into a four foot wash out. The trail down doesn't have a cow track on it. I put a little more slack in my reins and smooch Cante forward. "Let's go, bud."

Head low, Cante blows out a big breath and then takes one tentative step down. He shuffles forward, then his back feet slide down a foot. My buttcheeks clamp against the saddle leather as his front feet ease forward and his back ones slide down. Now we're looking up at the way out of here.

There's a little ledge a foot up the other side. Cante reaches it with one foot, and then his back feet are scrambling as the powdery dirt crumbles underneath them. I lean forward, give him his head, and pray. *Lord, get us out of here!*

Cante pushes up on the bank, breath puffing from his nostrils. I pat his neck and pant in the hot Texas air. "Good boy. Let's pick a different route on the way back."

I give him a minute to catch his wind before brushing my spurs against his sides, heading off in a trot. His gait is smooth and makes the two miles of nothing but prickly pear and greasewood pass by easily. There's fresh enough sign that bull has been around here in the last week, but definitely not the last couple of days.

Sweat slides down the whisps of hair that frame my face, and the sweet smell of a sweaty horse greets me with every little breeze. I pull Cante to a stop and scan the pasture for as far as I can see. Nothing.

I let out a sigh. "I hadn't figured on this taking all blooming day." Reigning around, I point Cante towards the fence. *Maybe he's gone visiting the neighbors.*

My mind wanders off as I study the fenceline for holes. The horse club has a sorting tonight.

Hopefully we make it. I pull my phone out of my leggins pocket and pull up James' text thread.

Do you have your horse ready?

The swooping sound of a sending message makes butterflies dance in my stomach, and for a second I wish there was an undo button.

It's supposed to be teasing. James will get that, right? I press the button on the side to darken the phone screen and slide it back in the leather pocket. In seconds it dings. A gray bubble with James' message is on the left side of the screen.

For what? Were we working cattle today?

I crack a grin. I can just see his eyes frantically flicking about, trying to recall the conversation where I'd asked him to help me with something. Only I didn't.

No. The sorting. Tonight. Arena at 7.

Ah, right. Nor, I've got things to do running out of my ears and Wade wants to go over numbers this afternoon. Maybe next time.

My shoulders slump. When we both worked for Wade, James was the one running around doing fun stuff while I was the hermit. Hard to believe that's changed.

I let out a sigh, glad James isn't here to see it.

Alright. Tell Wade hi for me.

Will do. I'm sorry .

No worries!

Sliding my phone back in my leggins, I pull Cante up and rein him around to face the same dry ground, sad mesquites, and tabosa cluttered cactus. I was very much not paying attention. I don't see any gaping holes in the fence though, so I put him back in a trot towards the corner.

No James at the sorting, but unless this bull hasn't made it very far there won't be a Nora either.

***

I snatch a couple cheese sticks and a half empty pouch of lunch meat from the fridge then shove on my worn black felt hat. After finding the bull in the neighbors' pasture, I'm going to be cutting it close to get waters checked and make it to the sorting. The back door creaks on its hinges as I drag it closed behind me.

The beat-up Chevy ranch pickup rattles to life, and dust puffs out of the vents. A cheese stick between my teeth, I shove the gear shift into second. A powdery cloud billows behind me. I make a point not to look in the lopsided mirrors at it.

There's more grass here than there was over at Wade's when I was calving heifers. I press my lips together in a thin line. These cows don't need me to help them calve like all those heifers, but if they did I wouldn't be running off to patch fence with Ian or join in on the sortings with the horse club.

I pull my water jug up from the passenger floorboard and slurp enough to wash the film of cheese off the roof of my mouth.

If James ever shows up to a sorting, I ought to ask him how number 94 is doing this year. A smirk cocks my lips, and I let it grow into a laugh. Like James is going to know which Hereford 94 is, let alone if she's calved or how she's doing. Hopefully she got bred back to one of Wade's bulls. They usually throw smaller calves. Smaller than that big black the neighbors to the east of us had.

A hole in the road nearly throws me across the cab. *Gahlee!* I've really got to fill that in before my head gets knocked against the roof. Or stop getting off in my own little world. That would be a solution too.

Little mesquites with vicious thorns screech against the doors as I veer off one two track road onto another. I follow the divots in a crescent, beside the long shallow cement trough. It's full, but I stop anyway. The float on this one has a tendency to lock up. I roll the big rock off the top of the thin sheet metal covering the float. I work the rod up and down a couple times before replacing the cover.

The corrosion would be worked out pretty quick if the cows used this part of the pasture. I've pushed them back here twice, but I guess the prickly pear in the front is better. The poor things haven't seen enough grass in their lives to appreciate the tubosa back here.

I wipe sweat from my upper lip and hop back in the cab. Off to the next one.

The Chevy squeaks the whole two miles to the wire gap. It's that ranch pickup squeak that sounds like it's in the seatbelt panel. No more than they get used, it probably is the seatbelts making the racket.

Pulling up to a wire gap that must be as old as the cement sheep waters, I sigh. It's a fight every time I open it. I get my arm around the square tubing of a post, wince in anticipation, and put all my weight against the post. The corners of the square metal hit nerves in my shoulder socket. I push harder. A grunt, and then I pop the wire loop off the top. *Before we move these cows out of here, I'm going to quit threatening and actually rebuild this.*

One leg hanging out the door, I pull through the gap. Putting it back up is the real chore. I pull a pickin' string out from behind the seat—the one I left the honda tied in the last time. Square tubing in the bottom wire loop, I pull the pickin' string around the fence post and tubing. Pulling for all I'm worth, I lift the top wire loop. With a squint and a grunt it slips on. "Whew!"

At the next water trough there's a couple of cows lounging in the shade. They stand as I push the pickup door open. One thin cow trots off several paces when I start for the reservoir.

"Quit your worrying. You'd gain more weight if you did." I step up on the two big rocks by the cement tank and peek over. Good and full.

Back in the pickup, I keep winding through the pasture to check two more troughs. Thankfully the patch I put on the one in the back held.

I string a bucket of feed out for the horses. I make Dune stand so I can run a hand down his dull red back. Several days ago he was pretty tender over his loin after a long day. It seems like he's worked the soreness out though.

While the horses clean up the feed, I hook my personal pickup onto my trailer.

Walking into the horse pen with a halter on my arm sends the three sorrels to the back corner. Heads high, they start down the fence. I step toward them and slap the lead rope on my leg. Banks faces me and bobs his head. "Thanks, bud, but I don't need you today."

Dune whirls back into the corner and snorts. Training my eyes on him, I hold the lead rope out to my right. "Hey, stand up there." He makes a dash for the other corner. Ears swiveling back and forth, he snaps to attention when I slap my leg again.

His neck is tight as I slip the halter up on his nose. "This is why you get to go tonight."

As soon as we take the first step to the barn, he blows out a breath and plods along behind me like an old plow horse. He cocks one back leg while I get him saddled. I toss the lead rope around his neck as he takes the first step in the trailer. I push the gate closed behind him and it screeches an ear piercing cry for grease. A hand still on the trailer, I look back at the other two in the pen. It sure would do Cante good to see town.

Ah, what the heck. I snag a halter from the saddle house wall and re-enter the pen. Cante doesn't move from beside Banks as I approach their corner, but he blows heavily through his nostrils as I halter him.

His steps do not relax until we're out of the pens. I tie Cante in the trailer and then fish Dune's rope. "Alright." I look up the trailer. "Let's go."

There are only a handful of pickups parked around the arena when I pull up. Cattle are already moving through the alley. George and Mindi—the backbone of the entire horse club—are putting numbers on the cattle.

I debate tying the boys to the trailer, but they'll stand just as well in it. Stuffing my hands in my pockets, I watch the ground as I stroll over to the alley.

"Afternoon," I call, though barely loud enough to be heard.

"Hey! Afternoon." George slaps a glue-covered paper number over the back of a yearling.

Mindi takes the glue cap out of her mouth. "Hey Nora, glad to see you."

"What can I help with?"

George looks around as Mindi hands him another number, and he backs up a couple steps to stick it on the next one. "We're just about done here. I think we've got it covered."

"Yes, I think we're good this time. Thank you!" Mindi squeezes on the glue tube, and it comes out on the paper in a burst. "How are those kiddos coming along?"

"Really great. They're all getting so much more confident!" I nod several times and feel the pull on my cheeks from smiling so wide.

Pickups and trailers start rattling up in lines, filling in the caliche field. Horses of every size, shape, and color start trotting around in circles, outfitted in every getup imaginable.

I nod in that direction. "I'm going to warm up the ponies. Let me know if y'all need anything." Gravel crunches under my boots as I step away.

Tied to the side of the trailer, Cante can't swivel his head or ears fast enough to take in all the commotion. I watch him a moment while I bridle Dune to make sure he's not going to pull any stupid stunts. It's just his ears moving, so I let Dune carry me through the maze with quick, but sure steps.

I've loped him in enough circles to get his head in the game by the time Mindi's voice rings through the microphone. She rattles off the first five or six teams. Dune and I are up pretty quick. This time with a short little man I've never met before. I usually tell Mindi I'll go with anyone who doesn't have a partner.

Riding up to the gate, I lick my lips and process words through my brain before trying to speak them. "Do you want to watch the gate, or sort?"

"I'll sort," he answers with a thick Spanish accent.

I nod once. *Alright, Dune, let's see how this goes.*

As soon as Mindi calls a number, the little man sinks the spurs into his gray mount and across the pen they squirt. The herd swirls into themselves. Perched on Dune in the middle of the two circular pens, I cringe and adjust my hands on the reins. *We're going to have to be on our game, bud.* My mount's ears swivel.

Three head come to us with the little man behind them. Dune's front feet start a dance. I try to read the numbers. We're starting with number eight.

Number eight is in the front, two others flanking him on either side. My whole body freezes, trying to decide which way for Dune to jump first. Before I can make up my mind, Dune makes it up for himself. He takes a big jump to the left. The number five yearling rolls back on its heels, but so does eight. Dune jumps to the right, turning three back to the herd and eight spins straight again.

The yearling trots through the gap. I settle myself back in the middle of the saddle with a little pat to Dune's neck. *Good boy.*

The next two yearlings the little man brings are the right numbers, but zero tries to come before nine. I poke Dune over to turn the wrong one back, but instead both of them turn straight into the little man.

I don't look up to see what he thinks about that. I just pull the side of my cheek in between my teeth and wait for the next yearling.

We won't get a no-time, cause the wrong one gets by. Not with Dune in the hole.

Chapter 3

Quack. Quack. Quack.

I swat at the bedside table. *How's it already time for the alarm?*

The quacking continues. I pry my eyes open and prop myself up on one elbow. Even with eyes open, my fingers fumble with my phone screen a couple times before I'm able to silence the alarm. I flop back against the pillow and yank the quilt over my eyes, my body melting back into the mattress.

I stir at the feeling of a line of drool on my cheek. My heart catches. How long have I been laying here for? Throwing back the covers, I snatch my phone up and read the blocky numbers at the top.

5:09. *Good thing I didn't sleep too long*

Wiping my cheek, I switch on the lamp and touch my bare feet to the gritty floor. *Rise and shine.*

Teeth brushed, I set the coffee pot to work. While it gurgles in the kitchen, I pilfer through my closet for the perfect shirt. One that makes me feel like a human.

I rub my eyes. I need all the help I can get with that today. One in the morning wasn't all that long ago. It was a fun night though. We round-robin-ed until everybody had been on a team with each other. My face relaxes as I shrug on an oversized blue paisley pearl snap.

Even though my jeans probably have salt stains from yesterday's sweat, I slide into them. It'll give Ian something to give me a hard time about. I can hear him now: "Your washer quit on you?" My lips cock a grin.

No, I just haven't worn them for a week straight yet.

Stopping by the coffee pot, I pour its contents on top of the cream in the bottom of my insulated mug and swirl it. *Perfect.* Every other step, I dare another sip of the scalding liquid like it's my functioning life-line. It kinda is.

The moon isn't even bright enough that I cast a shadow, but I know my way to the feed room. Inside the door, I flip on two light switches. One for the inside and one that shines out in the pens. I fill a five gallon bucket half full and step out the door to the soft nickers of my geldings.

Banks, roost ruler that he is, has his nose inches from the bucket all the way to the long trough in the middle of their pen. Dune and Cante play with one another behind him. I pour the feed down the length of the trough and squint at each of them in the remnants of light.

Trusty Banks's rich red coat shines, practically knick free. I guess the flies prefer duller reds, because they've sure been eating Dune's neck up. Sir Scaredy Cat Cante's hide shows evidence of the big boys getting fed up with him and taking a hunk out of it.

I traipse over to the pasture gate and tie it back against the fence. "Don't get into too much trouble."

My steps drag back to the house. Once inside the door, I take the lid off my mug and nearly down the rest in one gulp. It only burns my throat a little.

Before settling into my fluffy brown chair, I top off my mug with fresh coffee. The cushions welcome me in and I slide my worn Bible off the apple crates beside the chair.

The silk bookmark opens to James chapter two, and I read the first couple sentences under the *Faith and Deeds* heading. Taking a sip of coffee, I try to mull that over—take it beyond face value.

Can such faith save him?

Leaning my head back against the chair, I start a silent prayer.

God, things are going pretty good right now, and I have the tendency to wander off into my own world without you when things are going good.

Heaviness settles into my bones, and my eyes droop.

Lord, help me not to wander off without you during this good season. I don't want to just use you as a vending machine when times get rough.

Next thing I know, I'm jerking to life with a dried out mouth. Dadgummit! I fell asleep.

I'm sorry Lord. I'm off to a real good start on staying in communication with you, aren't I?

I gulp a drink of coffee, only for it to be cold. Scrunching up my face, I set my Bible back on the crates and stand. Clearly I'm not going to get much praying done in that chair. I peek at the kitchen clock and mutter under my breath. Then I grimace. *Wow, apparently I should try staying out late more often. It really brings out the best in me.*

"God, looks like you're already answering that prayer. I'm going to need a little help just to get to Ian's on time, let alone make it through the day decently."

I put my mug in the sink, flip off the light, and head for the door. I haven't been late to Ian's since Clay's cattle came in. Maybe there'll be other law breaking citizens on the road and we can all speed together.

The whole cab rattles, and the keys drop from the visor when I slam the pickup door. As soon as the engine rumbles to life, I crank it in gear, leaving dust in my path.

Oil field traffic this morning does not in fact feel like breaking the law. At least not the speed limit one.

Great.

We're supposed to be processing the cows Ian picked up yesterday so they can be turned out. Then we'll really see how good of a fence repairing job we did. Hopefully he hasn't started it by himself. Knowing Ian, he would.

A big truck scoots over into the little turning lane, and I punch it. In a few minutes, I flip on my left blinker and turn on the narrow road to Ian's. I swerve onto the little bit of a shoulder to not drop into the front-end-eater of a pothole. My front tire hits another pothole, tossing me against the door.

I grip the steering wheel till my knuckles are white and adjust back to the middle of the seat. It sure would be nice if the county got out and did something about these roads every once in a while.

Three curves and a dirt road later, I finally spot Ian and Denise's house. I glance at my phone for the time. The clock on the pickup is about as reliable as a half broke colt. I relax into the cracked leather seat. I made it within ten minutes of our meeting time.

Thank you, Lord! Ian already has enough reasons to tease me. I don't need to give him more.

I pull down by the saddle house and cut the engine. No rattling and banging comes from the pens behind it. That's a good sign. I adjust my hat a little lower on my head and slip through the saddle house door.

"Good morning, sorry I'm late," I sing out while my eyes adjust to the light.

"Hey!" Ian's deep voice bounces off the cinder block walls. The pale light from the fridge illuminates him.

"You didn't finish it all without me, did you?"

He chuckles and juggles three little bottles of cattle vaccines in one hand. "Not quite. How are you?" His opposite arm squeezes me in his signature bone crushing hug. Only this time it doesn't feel like my ribs could touch each other.

Weird.

I shrug it off and return the hug with as much power as I can muster. "I've been more awake before. We got a little bit too round-robin happy last night at the sorting."

"Sounds like I missed a good one then."

I reach for a medicine bottle that almost topples from his hands. "We'll be sure and carry out the full one a.m. experience when you make it to one."

He shakes his head, but a smile twinkles in his eye. "You kids."

Maybe he just couldn't squeeze as hard with all that medicine in his hand. But the hug and the nap the other day—it just doesn't add up.

I poke my head out the wooden door into the pens. "You did start without me."

Ian shakes his head, handing me a syringe. "I let them trickle up here through the night and threw out a bag of cake this morning. You didn't miss anything fun."

The syringe is stained a dirty brown color and sticks as I pull the plunger back. I drop it and the half-full bottle of medicine in the small ice chest in the doorway. Beside a pile of tools for the day. A Hot Shot, a couple branding irons, the branding pot, and a bottle of propane.

"What side of the chute—" I look up to point my question in the right direction, but somehow Ian has disappeared while I was preoccupied. One would think a big six foot man would be hard to lose, but I guess not.

He probably forgot something in the house. Hooking my fingers in the handle of the propane tank, I grunt a little when it lifts off the ground. Ian must have just topped it off. Even though I've got the hose up on my shoulder, the end of it still drags the ground as I lug the tank over beside the chute.

I grab the branding pot and set it up with the bottle. A high pitch screech from the chute bounces off the walls, trails off in a lower tone, and then is gone. I rub my temples, ears ringing. I guess wherever Ian went, he's back and ready to roll.

I turn the propane on just enough to hear it and then pick up the Hot Shot. Putting the tips on the homemade branding pot, I hold the button down and watch the tiny blue sparks tick out. It's not catching though.

I turn the propane on a bit more. Still not catching. I lift the Hot Shot away and turn the propane up to full blast. Muttering, I put the Hot Shot back on the cutout pipe and hold the power button down. Orange flames spray from the flame thrower into the branding pot.

Success! I lay both branding irons in the pot before turning away.

Back with the last armload of medicine and supplies, I breathe in the cloud of powdery caliche the cattle are stirring up milling in the tub. Surely Ian's cutting the calves off. Before I have time to ask him, his voice comes through the pipes.

"You got that Hot Shot?" Ian's hollers from across the pen.

I jump for the yellow rod and trot over to the metal pipes. Ian takes it, and I stand back out of the cows' sight while they decide to file up to the chute. In a minute, five of them are smashed up against each other while there's a three foot gap between them and the little gate Ian shuts.

I shake my head. These girls sure are living up to those tiger stripes down their backs. They're a little on the wild side.

Ian sets the catch gate on the front of the chute open just enough so they can see the light. Then he pulls up the little gate at the back of the chute, allowing the cows to step in. Reaching for the Hot Shot leaned against the fence, I step in behind the first cow.

Ian's cat-like reflexes snaps the catch gate snuggly on either side of her head. Her hooves hit the smooth metal sides of the chute in her flailing around. One pull of a handle brings the sides tight against her, and she settles down just a hair—until I stick a needle in her neck and the red hot iron touches her shoulder. She bellers, but in a second she twitches that skin and doesn't even flinch when Ian puts the iron back on to smooth it up. He pokes a flashy yellow ear tag into her ear while I give the other two shots. Then out the front she goes, with the same flying feet that she came in with.

Nearly all of them come into the chute the same way—front end off the ground, feet scratching the chute floor for traction, and then a sudden stop with their big ears flopping against the paint-chipped chute.

I drop the syringes in the ice chest and rest a hand on my hip. "Are you going to turn these girls out today?"

Ian rolls the iron up on an edge before looking over with a smug grin on his face. The same grin he gives me before doing something that's going to scare the crap out of me. "Don't you think they'd be fun to gather?"

I shake my head. "They're going to be fun enough after you ride through them for about a week."

A laugh bubbles from him as he clicks a tag into the cow's ear. "I'll leave them in that five acre lot and ride through them. I can spread hay out a little better for them and keep them from getting too stir crazy in a pen."

I slide the needle beneath her floppy hide and insert the medicine in. "That'll be good." *I hope that thing has six strand fences. New ones.*

I step back to let another one shoot into the head gate. Ian snaps an ear tag into her ear.

I turn to the chute with the branding iron just in time to see the tagging pliers fly towards the ice chest, and Ian duck around the corner of the saddle house.

For a moment time stands still and so do I, frozen halfway between the branding pot and the cow in the chute. *What just happened?*

I look at the taggers on the ground then swing my gaze to the corner of the saddle house. After dropping the iron back in the pot, my strides eat up the ground. I crane my neck around the corner of the saddle house before my body makes it around.

Ian leans up against the cinder block wall. I swallow the stickiness in my mouth. "You alright?" The words slip out just above a whisper.

A couple more light steps and I lay my hand on his shoulder squatting next to him. I lick my lips and try to get words to stop swimming in my head and actually become vocal. "Are you, um, okay?"

His big hand covers my knee, and he gives it a little squeeze. "Dee may have been right." Ian lifts his hat from its perch on his salt and pepper hair and tilts his head down. "Last night she pointed out the yellow tint on my forehead. This morning it's moved down on my chest too."

The breath that should be in my lungs has balled up in my throat. "That's not good." The words are almost inaudible and feel stupid as soon as they leave my lips. How's someone *supposed* to reply to these kinds of things?

Hat back on his head, he picks up a stick and pokes a rock around the pale dirt. "I haven't upchucked more than a half dozen times in my whole life until the last week."

And here we've been all day in the sun fixing fence. I let out a heavy breath between half parted lips, shoulders drooping. "You look a little pale. Let's go up to the house."

He glances over his shoulder as if he can see through the cinderblock wall.

I stand, offering him a hand up. "I'll turn the propane off. You head up to the house and I'll meet you there." I *wasn't* imagining the weakness of his hugs.

What if I'd said something about it?

But as he disregards my hand and stands on his own I know that *what if*—he would have waved it off.

I watch his weighted steps until he's several yards out the gate. He didn't even try to argue with me; this is bad.

I jog to the branding pot and turn off the propane. The cow in the chute—did she get all the shots yet? I stick her with them for good measure and then open the front for her. She sends flakes of dried poop flying behind her as she leaves.

I open the little rear gate and back the three cows out of the narrow alley. After closing the gate back, I take a look at the propane bottle and leave it all sitting right there.

I'm no runner, but the lack of air in my lungs has to do with more than just the run to the house. What's wrong with Ian? *A whole week of this.* Why'd it take me so long to notice?

Hand grasping the door knob, I take in a couple of calculated breaths, begging my lungs to accept the oxygen. I turn and push the door in. Quiet voices float around the corner, so I halt in the utility room.

"I think you need to go see a doctor about this, Dear."

"Dee." There's defeat in Ian's voice. Two sounds that don't belong together.

My heart crumbles. I take a few more light steps forward and run my thumbnail up the calluses of my index finger.

Ian's leaning against the kitchen counter. His eyes flick up to mine for half a second and then drop back to the floor. "You don't have to linger in the doorway."

Squaring my shoulders, I take a few more steps forward. Denise's forced smile makes me bite my lip. Like a bad movie getting worse, I watch two words form on Ian's lips.

"Let's go."

Denise and I both stare at him. For a moment, time is frozen, each of us looking at the other. Then Denise's throat bobs, and she splits to their bedroom. Ian ducks in the bathroom in the hall and I shuffle in the narrow pantry door.

Food. It's the only helpful thing I can think of.

I have a grocery sack half full of every type of snack they could possibly want when Ian plops his water jug on the counter.

"I hate to ask you, Nora—"

My eyes flicker from the lopsided *I* he carved into that jug. "I'll take care of them," I answer before he can ever finish the question.

He looks up, and I meet his eyes for a moment longer than usual. I swallow the fear that threatens to make my heart fly.

"Don't worry about marking the calves. We'll get them later."

I pluck at a string in the bottom of my jean pocket. "You take care of yourself. I'll handle things here."

Ian opens his arms and his face lifts just a little bit. "Thank you, girl." He crushes me in a hug—a real Ian hug—and I wonder if it hurts him.

I give him a pretty good squeeze of my own, but I hold back just a little bit. I'm not convinced he's alright yet.

"Okay." Denise's shrill voice bounces off the sunlight walls. "I got you a change of clothes, a phone charger, and your shoes in case your feet get tired in your work boots."

I study the resigned look on Ian's face. I force my eyebrows from their slump, but the weight in my chest must be tied to them too. "That's great. And I got y'all some snacks." I take hold of Ian's water jug. "Let me top that off for you."

Denise's voice shakes a little as she says, "Nora, do you mind checking on the dogs? I don't know how long we'll be gone, and I haven't fed them yet."

I screw the lid back on Ian's now full water jug. "Of course."

Bag in one hand, keys in the other, Denise scans the kitchen. Her gaze rests on her husband, but he's staring out the kitchen window. She draws in a breath, like she has to gather courage. "Ready, dear?"

He nods once, eyes glazed, like he's a million miles away.

"I'll take care of things here and see y'all up there as soon as I'm done." I hope my voice says what my words can't. *I'm sorry; I wish this wasn't happening; please be okay.*

I follow them out the back door. Denise goes on about how much she feeds each Aussie, but all her words go in one ear and out the other. I paste on a courtesy smile as the dusty red car door closes her in and Ian folds in the passenger side.

The engine starts, and the wheels roll backwards. I raise a hand in awkward recognition of their leaving.

White dust clouds up behind Denise's little red SUV, blocking it from my view long before they round the curve in the road. I watch until the dust is gone, then I drag myself back to the pens.

I start the propane with the Hot Shot again. While the irons are heating up, I take the little yellow stick and climb on the side of the tub. The cattle mill again, all crammed up against one another in the tightest ball they can manage.

As much as I want to get this done and leave, I don't poke them with the Hot Shot. I just throw one leg over the top of the fence and perch. Mentally, I retrace every single thing I've done in the last week.

Monday and Tuesday I was here. *What did I miss?* Something was wrong with Ian right before my eyes, and I missed it.

I shake my head. Maybe if I hadn't been thinking about the kids's next playday or how to con James into going to the sorting I would have noticed.

A cow steps through the small gate, sniffing the pipes on each side of her. I hold still, and in a minute she's moved up and has a friend following her.

Ian's yellow skin, throwing up, naps.

Another cow files in, and then a fourth. Leaning up as far as I can reach, I touch the third one with the Hot Shot without pressing the button. She jumps forward like I did let the electricity out. With her moved up, a fifth cow files in the back, and I squeeze the gate closed behind them.

I jump from the fence, landing on my feet, but my ankles scream at me. Paying them no mind, I set the catch gate and lean back against the rope to let a cow up. Thankfully she's a little less flighty than the others have been, and I manage to get it closed with her head still in it.

She shakes her head, throwing snot around, when I give her a bright yellow ear tag. By the time I've given her shots and two brands, she really is slobbering everywhere. I turn her loose, and she trots off to the middle of the herd.

One down, fifteen more to go.

When all the cows have been processed, I run water through the syringes and put everything back in the corner of the saddle house. I open the gates to the water lot and let the cows go back to any scraps of hay that are left.

At the water hose by the saddle house, I rinse the dust out of my mouth and then drink a few slurps. With all the excess running down it, my face gets a cleaning too. Just before turning the water off, I rub my hands under the stream and then dry them on the bottom of my worn jeans.

Standing in the door of my pickup, I reach around the steering wheel and crank the engine. I scan my surroundings. Cows are turned back, no horses are tied, and everything's put away. I nod once and jump into the Chevy.

The dogs! I told Denise that I'd feed them.

Putting the pickup in reverse, I turn around and back right up to the kennels. I barely have enough room to slip out between the door and the cab the side of the pen is so close.

Little round food pellets fall into bowls on each side of the kennel. I look over each water bucket. They're three quarters full or better.

"See you later," I mumble and turn again for the pickup.

Windows down, I circle out of the drive and head for Midland. Even though I know there's plenty of holes in the road, I put the gas to it. If I mess up Clay's already worn out pickup, I'll gladly pay the repairs. I just need to get to the hospital.

I look at my phone. Nothing. By now they should at least be there, if not in a room. I drop it back on the seat beside me, and it bumps against the butt of my pistol stuffed between the seat cushions. Denise said she'd tell me as soon as they know something. My fingers tap on the steering wheel and my knee bounces. *Waiting sucks.*

Ian in the hospital. I saw him leave in the car for it, but I still can't get the puzzle pieces to line up. The man's invincible. That's why he always scared me as a kid.

Off the dirt road and onto the FM. The roads don't get better, but I push the old pickup for more. I want to be there. I *need* to be there. To know what's going on.

I'm to the edge of the big town crawling with people on their way to do who knows what when my phone buzzes. I snatch it from the seat and glance between the words and the road until I have the message read.

According to Denise, they've done a sonogram, and there's a stone over his bile duct. That's why he's yellow. *Jaundice* is actually the word Denise uses.

It could be worse, I guess.

As soon as I pull into the hospital parking lot, I find a spot in the boonies. I job the lock down on the passenger door, then my own. Boot heels clipping on the pavement, I take off for the hospital doors.

I can smell the chemicals burning my nose hairs out before I even get inside. *How on earth do people work in these places?* By the time the automatic doors slide apart, I'm pretty sure I don't have a sense of smell anymore.

I scan the ER waiting room with its blue padded chairs and people sitting in clusters. Making my way to the desk behind a plastic wall, I try to get my words to string into sentences.

The nurse looks up, and a peachy little smile parts her lips. *Is that all the sanitary chemicals getting to her head?*

"What can I help you with?"

I smile back, though there aren't any peaches with mine. "I'm looking for Ian Kelly."

She rifles through some papers. "Do you have your ID on you?"

I dig it out of my pocket and hand it over with clammy hands.

She scans it and nods. "It looks like he's in the second room here on the left. I'll let you in the door beside the window."

"Thank you."

She leaves the little plastic window, and in a second the door swings open. I tuck my hands in my pockets and tiptoe through like the shiny tiles might give way.

The pale hall walls are made a little brighter with posters in little kids' handwriting. *You're doing great! Get better soon! You're a rock star!* I only read a couple of them before I'm at the second door.

The knob is cool in my sweaty hand. I hold it for a moment before finally letting myself inside. Ian paces the little room like a caged animal. His eyes meet mine, and I swallow. They're not shiny white around his crystal blue irises. "Hey, girl."

My smile becomes a little more real as I wrap my arms around his middle. "Hey," I croak. I give Denise a hug too and pat her shoulder.

"Thanks for coming," she says.

"Of course." I look around the tiny room with bland gray walls. Between the bed in the middle, a chair just inside the door, and cabinets in one corner there's hardly enough room to turn around. "So what do they tell you they're going to do for this pesky little rock?" The bright, cheerful words I was going for come out sounding foreign.

Ian huffs and sinks onto the stiff hospital bed. "They'll take it out in the morning. The doctor that's going to do it is on vacation."

Denise's hands fidget with one another. "They're getting a room upstairs for him."

I lean against the cabinets and grip the countertop. "That's good."

"I guess," Ian mumbles, looking down.

The beeping of some alarm outside winds up Ian's pacing again. It's starting to get me jumpy too. Denise looks slumps into the single chair.

I look around, trying to find some cute sign on the wall to read or grains of wood to study. There are none. Only drab tasteless walls.

I cross my ankles and then uncross them. This place even feels like a cage for me. "Are they at least letting you eat tonight?"

He glances up at the clock on the wall. "For a few more hours anyway."

"What do you want to eat? Tell me where and I'll go get it."

I can breathe and they can have some good food.

Chapter 4

I sink into the pickup seat, breathing in some real air instead of that sanitized stuff. My hat plops on top of the heap of tools in the passenger side, and I lean my head back. The sun blinds me through the windshield, but it won't erase the image from my mind. That haunted look in Ian's eyes.

I can't get it out of my head.

Pinching the bridge of my nose, I swallow away the burn in my throat. *He's going to be okay.* The surgery should be pretty minor, and he'll be back on his feet shortly.

I wipe the sweat from my upper lip, crank the window down, and start the engine. A water line part from the heap in the bench seat pokes my ribs as I lean across and wind the passenger window down. I just take the jab though. Beats getting out and walking around.

A glance at the towering building with all its shiny windows reinforces the weight on my chest. I put the pickup in gear and head east for the nearest Blue Sky burger place.

The streets are swarming with people out to lunch. I turn onto what looks like a quiet little side street, but within two stop signs, there's cars zipping past me. By the time I make it to the burger joint, all I can smell are exhaust fumes.

I pull the little paper with our order from my back pocket and walk in. The instant buzz of voices all talking at once is overwhelming. Do people really do this everyday?

"How can I help you, ma'am?" A short blonde girl calls out from behind the register.

"Can I place a to-go order, please?"

"Sure!" She taps the computer screen a few times. "Okay what can I get you?"

I rattle off the three orders. Ian and Denise are trying one of their fancier burgers. I just get bacon on mine and call it good. Burgers are made to be simple. That's why I like them.

"What name can I put on that for you?"

I swallow. "Kelly."

The little blonde grins. "We'll have that right out for you."

I try to return the bright smile she has, but I don't think I do a very good job. "Thank you." Stepping aside for the next person, I nearly knock the fake plant over. My cheeks are flaming as I straighten it and make a bee-line for the restroom in the corner of the room.

A hand on each side of the sink, I squeeze my eyes shut. Just a few days ago we were fixing fence for eight hours straight. How'd we get here? I throw a little water on my face.

I've been keeping up with sortings and the playday kids, but I can't keep up with the man that saved me from ending up behind a crop insurance desk right now.

I step back and my hands shake at my sides. *What have I come to?*

The door squeaks open, and a little ten-year-old girl peeks in. I turn the water off and snatch a couple paper towels as her mom follows. Grabbing the towels signals the automatic dryer, and it makes enough racket to drown out the restaurant chatter. I wipe at my hands, toss the towels in the trash, and duck out the door.

The line by the register has thinned a little, and I find a piece of wall to hold up while I wait. I run one fingernail under another over and over and over again. I hit too deep, sending a pain wave up my finger. Biting the inside of my lip, I shove my hands into my tight front pockets that are hardly deep enough to hide my top knuckles.

The blonde behind the counter scurries from who knows where and back again. As she moves, her tennis shoes squeak against the grungy floor.

Eyes fixed on the swinging glass door, I feel my throat try to close up.

The squeaky shoes appear in front of my blurred vision. I swallow and press my lips into that smile again. The fake one.

"Here's those burgers for you. The drinks are on top."

My fingers clasp around the plastic handles of the bag. "Thank you."

"Have a good day."

Good day. I wish today could be one. "You too."

I prop the food up in the passenger seat, tucking a rolled up denim jacket around it to keep it standing up. Before I jump in the driver's seat, I roll the off side window down. If I would have known I would end up here when I left the house this morning, I would have brought my personal pickup. At least it has electric locks and windows. Not to mention an air conditioner.

At a stoplight my phone buzzes. I turn it over and get half the text read before the car in front of me takes off. Turning the phone screen-down on the seat, I press on the gas.

Ian's in an actual room now. Denise went into all kinds of detail as to what parking lot to park in and which door to use in her text.

I switch lanes and take a right onto the little backroad I found on the way out. I hardly know what direction is what, much less the street names.

Between one way streets and signs with confusing arrows, I have to make a couple blocks before I get to the right entrance to what I think is the correct parking lot. Again, I don't even try to find a spot close to the door. I don't feel like trying to fit this big pickup in a box for a toy car.

In fact, I don't feel like leaving this cab at all. And at the very same time, if I stay out here another minute I'll go crazy.

If I just lay eyes on Ian maybe there won't be a thing wrong with him, but I know it's not true. I push the truck's door open and plant my boots on the asphalt. There's nothing I can do to change things. And that's the worst part.

I grip the bag of takeout, shoulders slumping like it's ten times heavier than it is, and strike off for the hospital doors. Before reaching the entrance, I take the drink carrier off the top of the sturdy to-go boxes. It makes me feel better, something in each hand, like I'm doing more. Mighty small comfort.

The doors roll open with a squeak. I nod with a pressed smile at a man pushing a stroller. Newborn babies must be the only reason that anyone is around a hospital and happy. They'll light up the greyest day—like newborn calves.

Signs point me to the elevator. It groans right before finding the fourth floor and the doors open. I step out and force my chin up.

Four-fifty-five, four-fifty-seven, four-fifty-nine.

I slap on a smile, beg it to replace the worry in my eyes, and push on the door. I'm hardly three steps into the room before Ian's curling his fingers around the plastic bag. I shake my head with a little bit of a truer smile taking over my lips. It's the most foreign image, Ian in the hospital. But at least for a moment he's still my Uncle Ian.

"Burgers and what they claim to be the best iced tea in town." I hand Ian a big cup with a straw on top as he sets the sack on the end of the bed. "You be the judge."

Denise takes the styrofoam boxes out of the bag. "Y'all sip on that tea, I got a burger calling my name."

I grin a little. Actually, food does sound pretty good. I hadn't given it a second thought until now. I take the box Denise offers me and slip to the back corner of the room. Perching on the window sill, I beg the hand that has a hold of my lungs to relax, even just a little bit.

Ian sets his cup on the little hospital table. "I haven't tasted the rest of the town's tea, but this isn't too bad."

"Oh good." I kinda already forgot about the tea.

A couple bites into my burger, there's a little knock at the door and a nurse comes in. She gives Ian a once over. "Glad to see you have an appetite, Mr. Kelly."

His lips twitch to one side, a little guilty. The burger in his hand is laid down in its box.

She holds up a green gown. "Doc wants you in this in the next couple of hours. You're welcome to keep your Wranglers on if that makes you more comfortable." A little nervous laugh bubbles out of her.

His fingers brush against the bottom of his jeans. "Yes ma'am."

"Alright, I'll be back in a bit to check on you." She stalls. "Just make sure you're done eating by midnight."

Denise smiles at her from the chair by the bed. "Thank you."

My burger goes dry in my mouth. The silence is nauseating: the fry that was halfway down my throat threatens to come back up. This surgery in the morning is like a dark cloud looming. We're just waiting to see how bad it hits.

No. I close my eyes for a second and then swallow. The food stays down, but I tuck the fries into the paper bag and roll the top down anyway. Before I can gather up the trash, Denise reaches for my napkins and steps outside to drop them in the hallway trash can.

Ian pivots on the bed. "How'd the rest of those cows do?"

I hold back a chuckle, because it wouldn't be a lighthearted one. I think we become more alike everyday. And it's scary. "Good. I got all of them caught the first time they came through."

He's perched on the side of the bed, set to spring into pacing at any moment. It's just his eyebrows that launch right now though. "Look at you go."

"I just put them back there where they were. Tomorrow I'll go over and tend to them, get them settled."

He stares at the wall like he'll cut a hole in it and leave. I watch his throat bob. Then he looks at me. "Thank you."

All I do is nod in response.

What he doesn't say says it all.

***

By the time we've walked the halls enough times my legs ache, and I've assured Ian and Denise that I don't mind tending to things in the morning, it's getting pretty close to my bedtime. The old Chevy's headlights barely light up the two lanes let alone the bar ditches. I prop up against the window sill and let the night air whip my hair into knots I'll regret tomorrow.

Tomorrow. It can't come fast enough. And then be over with, so that we can get on with life. How it is supposed to be.

I clamp my hand around the steering wheel as emotions take hold of my throat. *Gosh, I'm so tired of tight throats and tears in my eyes.*

My phone lights up on the seat beside me. A text from Mindi.

All three of your playday kids are already signed up for this first one. Thank you so much for coaching them!

My heart's already so low it can't drop anymore. The first horse club playday of the season is a week away. Six days to sort through everything running through my mind and be a sane human.

That's awesome! We've had some family things come up that should be good to go by then, but I'll let you know.

My eyes glaze over, seeing the road and yet not registering mile after passing mile. There's just the hum of the tires on asphalt and the weight of worrying and waiting. It's several minutes before my phone buzzes again.

I hope everythings okay. No worries if you can't make it Saturday.

I let off the gas and put on my blinker before rumbling across the cattle guard to the house. I don't want to let those kids down, but if it's between Ian and a playday it'll be Ian every time.

Making a pass by the pens, three sets of eyes glow in the headlights. My geldings have come up for a treat. "Hang around until in the morning," I mumble, parking by the house.

I stumble over the worn path to my front door, turn the knob, and give the paint-chipped door a shove with my shoulder. The familiar musty feel welcomes me. Much better than that sterile stuff. On my way by, I flick on the switch above the stove. It sheds just enough light so that I don't stub my toe on the doorframe as I step into my bedroom.

Snatching my pajamas from under my pillow, I keep going for the bathroom. I'm exhausted clean through my bones, but I don't think I'll be sleeping much. I turn the shower on and imagine the water driving my whirlpool of thoughts away. If only that was possible.

Too bad I don't know someone who's calving heifers right now. If I'm not going to sleep anyway I could at least do something productive while I worry.

Chapter 5

Two, four... six bags of feed on the old Chevy. With a sack on my left shoulder, I pull the roller door down with my right and move the latch in place with my toe. I sling the sack onto the pickup bed and jump in the driver's seat. I turn my phone over to see the screen. It's blank. I rub my hand on my jeans and fish the keys out from under the console.

No news is good news, they say, but I'm not at all convinced. It's been hours since Denise texted that they were taking Ian back for the surgery. I start the Chevy and slip it into gear. I thought he was just having a little procedure and it wouldn't take too long.

The front tire drops into that hole I've been meaning to fill up for weeks now. It tosses me against the door and launches my phone to the floor. I brake too hard and throw myself against the steering wheel.

Righting myself, I fold myself into the floorboard to retrieve my phone. Cringing, I let off the clutch and ease down the two tracks again. This time I manage to skirt around the biggest holes. The mesquites scrape against the sides of the Chevy through the middle of the draw behind the house. I coast around the bend beyond it and come upon the first water trough.

I check my phone again, but still nothing from Denise. I shove the pickup door open, dust wafting in the cab as I take the couple strides to the reservoir.

A handful of cows are grazing on either side of the road. After a couple wails of the siren, a steady trickle of them amble up to the pickup.

I step out of the cab, and half the cows scatter in the bushes a hundred yards out. The rest of them peer on across the water trough. From the bed of the pickup I can see over the scrub brush to count them. Forty-seven here. The pasture is only supposed to have forty-five.

A dry chuckle leaves my lips and I jump down to the ground. *Something's always got to be where it doesn't belong.*

I fiddle with the string on the end of the feed sack and then try the other end. Finally it comes loose and I pull it about halfway back. I sling one arm around the end of the bag while the opposite hand takes hold of the corner.

The cows run off a couple paces then turn to watch me with heads held high. A few inch up to the line of cake farthest from the pickup as I walk back. I string out two more sacks, flustering the cows each time.

Empty sacks tucked under the full one, I drive off. My chest feels just a little bit lighter. Maybe my head's a little more in the game, too.

I cock myself in the seat to rest my arm out the window. Instead of calling up the West Field cattle, I hit the FM road and head for Ian's. His cattle need hay this morning. Denise might like a couple pictures of her dogs too.

From the little rise in the road before the house, I squint down at Ian's. I don't let myself put on the brakes and stew on it. *He'll be back in those pens in no time.* For now, I'll hold them down for him.

Denise's little aussies yap over the purr of the motor before I get it turned off. I stick my fingers through their pens and let the dogs lick them for a second. "I'll be back."

Rocks blur under my feet as I head for the skid steer. I dig around the cubby beside the seat until I fish out a flathead screwdriver. The machine hasn't had a proper key since I've been coming around. Wedged in the groves just right, the screwdriver turns the motor and it rumbles to life. A piece of metal clanks on the side of the box. It's probably supposed to be welded or bolted somewhere, but hey it's still running. The brain scrambling sound dies down a little out from under the beat-up tin shed.

The skid steer bumps over to the rows of round bales. I run the hay spikes into the first bale and lift it high enough to see under it. I start for the water lot, but stop after a couple rolls of the tires. Ian wanted them in the trap and the hay rolled out. I glance in toward the trap. Surely I can get over here with a horse tomorrow to ride through them like he wanted. He probably shouldn't be horseback for a while.

I nod once to myself and start bumping away to the trap. Before getting the trap gate I pull out my phone, but the screen only holds that picture of my three geldings and the time across the top in big white numbers.

Denise said it should only be a couple hours tops. We're going on three. I slip my phone in my shirt pocket. He's probably just in recovery and she hasn't had time to call.

Patience, Nora. I've never had much of that.

In the middle of the trap, I cut the netting off the bale and use the spikes to roll it a quarter of a turn at a time. On the way out I rev the throttle up to bunny speed.

My hands still vibrate a little bit when I step down. This time when I pull my phone out there's two notifications. The little phone inside a green square with Denise's name beside it.

A voicemail. My chest grabs itself like a half broke colt.

I force air out between my teeth and lift the phone to my ear. Her voice starts to roll. Even before she gets past the first two words my throat squeezes and my eyes burn.

"Hey Nora." Two words I never thought could be so heavy.

"The surgery didn't go like the doctor had hoped. It's not a stone. It's a tumor, and there's a spot on his liver. He biopsied it, but won't know anything for several days."

There's a pause in the message. I squeeze my eyes together.

"So long as he comes out of anesthesia okay, we'll be home tonight. Talk to you soon, bye."

I lean against the battered tin wall of the machine shed. Taking my hat in my hands, I curl the brim in my fist.

A tumor. *And* a spot.

I force air into my lungs. It can't be good if the doctor didn't just take the tumor out while he was already there.

One word that no one has said. One word is all that it'd take to completely shatter the thread of hope that I—we all—are clinging to. I swallow it away before my brain can actually register that C word.

Taking out my phone, I type out a message. Guilt sits heavily on my chest that I missed the call, and now I'm too weak to return it. But I know my voice is anything but normal right now and that's not what Denise needs.

I got your message. Thanks for it. Do y'all need anything? I'll take care of everything here.

Slipping the device back in my pocket, I drag myself down the alley to the cattle. *Better get these girls on some hay.* A cow throws her head up and blows snot as I open the water lot gate.

I close my eyes and swallow. *Not today, Momma. Please.*

I ease around the fence, keeping an eye on her. A calf on the other side of the lot starts nosing its way toward the gate. *Good, at least someone has some sense.*

Slowly squatting down, I pick up a good-sized white rock and hold it at my side. That same momma cow is still staring me down. She's pivoted almost in a whole circle to keep me in her sights. The other cows are halfway out the gate, and her baby has decided she'll go with them.

Her head lifts. I jostle the rock in my hand. "Go on! Your baby's got more sense than you do," I growl.

She tosses more snot. I throw the rock hard enough it feels like my arm might go with it. It pings the side of the water trough in front of her before plopping inside of it.

One more toss of her head, and then she turns. As if her eyes have been opened to a whole new world, she picks up a swinging trot and follows the rest of them up the alley.

Amazing what happens when you pay a little attention.

A buzz comes from my cell in my pocket. I snatch it so fast it almost flies out of my hand. What would Denise be calling about now? Is everything okay?

As I read the name on the screen, I blink and bite my lip. *Clay.*

"Hello?"

"Hey Nora, how are things going?" His voice is crisp like his white lawyer's shirt.

I lean against an alley post, picking at the splintered wood. "It's going." He may be friends with Ian, but spouting off my uncle's problems isn't something I'm doing.

"Good, good. How are the calves growing out?"

I rolls my eyes and chip a piece off the post. "Pretty good. The grass is holding out since the last rain."

"Good..." The word dragged out a little. "I don't think I have updated counts. Will you send me a picture of yours?"

My eyes glance at the Chevy at the end of the alley. "Yes sir, I'll get those to you here in a bit."

"How's your 'ole uncle doing?"

My shoulders jerk to attention. A ball of lead forms in my throat. "He's... getting along." The words come out halted. "You ought to holler at him."

"Sounds like I ought to." A scraping noise muffles his words, like maybe he's scratching the stubble on his jaw. "Well, I've got a meeting to get to. Holler at you later."

I mumble my parting words and tap the red *end call* button. My sweaty fingers slip across my phone case, and I catch it just before it hits the ground.

Did I just lie to him? Caliche crunches under my feet as I set myself in motion. It can't be a lie if no one knows how he's actually doing.

***

The little red car races the cloud of caliche, getting passed as it rattles over the cattle guard. The dust floats to me, tickling a cough out of my throat. The little Aussie in my arms tries to wiggle free while yapping right up next to my ear. I keep a hold of it only by a handful of the loose skin behind its neck.

The car rolls to a stop in the bits of gravel close to the back door. The driver's door is the first to open, and Denise's light brown head of hair appears. What seems like several minutes, but probably only seconds later, the passenger opens.

As he rises from the seat, Ian slips his black felt hat onto his head. His eyes find mine, and his lips manage a smile.

I let the wiggling dog loose, and it bounds toward Denise. With each step, my legs become steadier as I reach Ian. But Denise intercepts me in the front of the car, and I wrap my arms around her.

No words are exchanged, and I'm glad. Hopefully my hug can say more than I'd ever find words for. I let her go and take a few steps to Ian. His hug is more like the ones I've come to expect from him than the last several I've gotten. I let myself squeeze him a little tighter than I think his body should be squeezed.

The three of us take several shuffles toward the house before Denise breaks the silence. "Well, they sent him enough pills home that it'll be a meal all by itself."

I cock my lips in the best smile I have. "I'm sure it'll taste about as good as my cooking."

"Hey now." Ian gives my shoulder a playful shove. "A home cooked meal sounds great, regardless."

I grab the door with trembling fingers, motioning for them to enter before me. "There's cornbread, beans, and some ground beef warm on the stove."

"Thank you, Nora." Denise's voice can barely be heard over the gust of wind that rattles through the yard.

I put my hand on her shoulder and then draw my hand away. I never know how to time the comforting touches like she does. "Of course."

Inside the door, my aunt and uncle sink into chairs. Ian on a bar stool in the kitchen. Denise makes it into the living room to one of the big leather chairs. Weariness creases in the space between their eyebrows.

I busy myself by putting away the dishes that I'd washed while I was waiting on them to get here.

"How are the cows settling in?" Ian wastes no time getting to business.

I smile and stop my piddling. Leaning back against the sink, my hands find my front pockets. "They seem a little less on edge since they can sneak off into the mesquites in the corner."

The ghost of a smile appears on his lips. "Sounds about right."

The quiet takes over again for several minutes. Then he nods at the pots on the stove, hauling himself to his feet. "That stuff is smelling pretty good."

I jump to get a plate. "I'll get it for you." Grasping the big spoon beside the stove, I plop a heap of beans and beef on his plate. Then I frame the plate with two pieces of cornbread.

Ian takes the portion with wide eyes and a playful smile. "Afraid I'm going to blow away are you?"

My hands play with each other and I force my eyes not to look away. "Just precautionary measures."

He takes a forkful to his mouth and bites off cornbread with it. A few crumbs stick to the ends of his mustache. "It's good," he says, filling another fork full.

I move a tiny rock across the floor with the toe of my boot. "Thank you."

Denise pads into the kitchen. She dishes out half a spoonful of beans and beef on her plate. Perching on a stool across from Ian, she glances at me. "You eat too, Nora"

I push myself away from the counter and pick up a cool tin plate. At the very least, it'll give me something to do with my hands, but my stomach has started to voice its opinion too. I scoop about half as much as I did for Ian and pull up another stool to the end of the bar.

Several minutes pass with just the clink of utensils on plates. Finally, I swallow and wash the grub down with a gulp of tea. "What kind of laws did they give you to follow?"

"Rest." Ian says the word about as disgusted as he would have said *ticks*.

I chuckle a little. "That's not too bad."

"They said they'll call in the next day or two with the biopsy results." All humor is gone from his voice, not even the sarcastic kind.

I try to push cheer onto my face, but it dies on my lips in seconds. "That'll be good."

Denise's eyebrows arch and she slides her plate in the sink. "Yes, it'll be good to know."

Ian retires to his big leather chair around the corner, but a heavy cloud lingers in the kitchen.

Helpless, I run a sink of soapy water and start scrubbing more dishes. Denise appears by my side to rinse them. "That biopsy's got him pretty sore."

I glance over my shoulder, as if I could see a frown deepening on Ian's face through the wall. "I bet it does."

Plates clink against one another in the sink. "We've crossed a lot of sketchy bridges. We'll get across this one, too." My eyes meet hers, and a peaceful smile pulls the edges of her lips.

I try to return the smile but drop my eyes. That's some kind of tough I don't think I have—to face something this big and just know you'll get through it.

Dishes finished, I search the corners of the kitchen for something else to keep my hands busy. The worn countertops have been wiped clean, stove sparkles right down to the propane burners, and I scrubbed the fridge minutes before Ian and Denise got back. Short of organizing the spices, I'm out of things to clean.

Denise sinks onto a bar stool.

"Do you need anything else tonight?" I start to put my arm around her, pull it back, then bite the inside of my cheek and do it anyway. I've got to get better about these hugs.

She leans against me a little and shakes her head. "No, sweetheart. Thank you though."

"Of course," I murmur, giving her shoulders a squeeze just as Ian does mine.

Rounding the corner, I watch Ian wrapping and unwrapping a piece of leather around his hand. I shuffle around the back of his chair to lean against the old wooden rocking chair across from him and fiddle my fingers around one another.

"What do you think?" Ian's voice is thick—tired.

I shake my head, baby hairs flailing on each side of my face. "Try not to do too much of that."

He holds the leather wrapped around his hand for a moment. "It is dangerous, isn't it?"

My thumb nail scrapes under my index fingernail. A moment passes. I lick my lips and force my words to work. "Everything at the pens is taken care of; I got the new cows out in the trap with hay."

"You're too handy, girl."

I lean down to give him a hug with a brush off chuckle. "Get some rest tonight."

He wraps his arms around my shoulders from where he sits and then looks deep into my eyes. "You, too."

I manage a smile and duck out the door, retreating from the house as fast as I can without looking like I'm actually fleeing. As soon as I'm in the Chevy, I drag in several deep breaths until it feels like oxygen is actually staying in my lungs.

Lord, take care of him.

Chapter 6

Steam wafts out of the top of my coffee mug as I carry it to my chair in the living room. Dim light filters in the south window. I sink into the chair and it groans. The thinning brown fabric rolls up under my socked heels as I pull my knees toward my chest.

Coffee scalds the back of my throat, but the mug between my hands soothes my heart. I release one of my hands to pull my Bible on my lap. The gold-edged pages flutter, and my mini-legal pad with yesterday's church notes falls out. The inky writing has smeared a little, but the reference is still readable.

1 Corinthians 12:12-31.

Another sip of coffee, this time a little gentler going down, and then I open the worn leather book to 1 Corinthians.

The first couple points I'd jotted down on the yellow lines just because they were on the screen, but the third one stuck out to me. From verse twenty-six: *we bear one another's burdens, so that it is spread out.*

I take a good swallow of coffee before relinquishing it to the side table and swiping the pen from beside it. I turn to a fresh page and touch the pen to paper.

Dear Lord—

My phone dings from across the room. Startling, I set my Bible aside. What if it's something with Ian?

But I keep myself in the chair. If it was something too important they'd call, and if I get up from here I won't finish reading this. I take a sip of coffee and look at the clock on the wall. Already eight-thirty.

I unfold the Bible in my lap again and read over my notes again. A pray forms in my mind like a plea.

I'm struggling to know how this applies to me. It seemed like you made it jump off the page to me yesterday, but I still haven't puzzled out why.

A page of scribbled prayers later, I re-read the whole passage. Maybe God will help me better understand as I go about my day.

In the few steps it takes to get to the table, and my phone, I down the rest of my almost cold coffee. My phone lights up as I turn it over, and the one line text from Ian pops up.

Will you swing by the house when you get a chance today?

My heart hangs in the balance. *If it was something urgent, he would have called me,* I remind myself.

I answer with a quick 'yes sir' and bee-line it for my boots. The heels click on the hardwood floors as I buzz around the house, turning the coffee maker off and gathering up my water jug and pistol.

I idle the Chevy over to the pens and throw some feed out for the sorrel trio. A dust cloud stirs up behind me on the way to the pavement.

Ian and Denise's house comes into view, and I veer left toward it instead of the pens. Should I knock? Ian usually just meets me at the saddle house, so I've never had to worry about it before. If he's resting I don't want to disturb him.

My hand rests on the wiggly doorknob. I take a deep breath and push the door open. It creaks, and I don't know whether to feel thankful it's announcing my presence or cringe that it's making too much noise.

I tiptoe across the stretch of the utility room floor that always whines, careful not to make much more racket. Ian probably *should* be sleeping, whether he is or not.

I make it around the corner to find Ian and Denise in the kitchen. They look at me and then each other. Denise moves to Ian's side and rubs a hand on his back. I stop in the doorway, and a question catches in my throat.

Ian slowly looks up to my eyes for a moment. If his face gets any paler, I might start thinking he hasn't met the sun. His eyes seem to have sunk back in his head overnight. I thought he was getting better.

Ian presses his lips into what wants to be a smile, but my heart plummets.

I look to Denise, but she's gone back to fiddling at the kitchen sink.

"Come on in." Ian opens his arms where he sits on a stool.

I coast around the end of the bar and stand next to him and lay my arm across his shoulders. His hangs loosely around me. Without command, my thumb rubs half circles on his shoulder. I want to tell him it'll all be alright. Instead I swallow away the panic.

"The doctor called." Ian's voice is strained.

My free hand stills by my side.

He runs a hand over his face. "It's not good."

Chest tight, I curl my fingers into my palm. *I knew that as soon as I walked in the door.*

His gaze is on Denise now. It lingers there for a long moment. Then it swings up to meet my eyes and hangs there, too. He squeezes me to him in a little hug and stands.

Ian's hands move to rest on Denise's shoulders, and his lips touch a light kiss to the top of her hair. The slow motion scene oozes into the words that leave his mouth: "The tumor is cancer and there's a spot on my liver."

My thoughts stop dead in their tracks. I reach for the bar to save me from crumpling.

"They called this morning. We'll go back to Midland in a few days."

I'm snapped back into functioning. My fingers interlace and I stare at them, rough and darkened with grime.

"I-I'll be here to take care of things." The words tumble out, and I can't believe they're the first thing I say.

I look up to find both of them staring at me. I press my lips together. "I'm sorry," It comes out in a whisper, and then I turn out the door.

My strides stretch long. I beg the bile in my throat to stay down. *Just a few more steps.* Jerking the pickup door open, I throw myself inside. My chest heaves air in and out without retaining any of the oxygen.

Cancer.

I finally let the C word fully develop in my mind.

I grip the steering wheel until I'm sure my fingers will stay wrapped around it forever. It's not just my heart that's broken; my whole chest is shattering. This can't be happening. It's just one awful nightmare that's been going on for days— weeks, probably.

Ian—Ian that has made both real estate and cattle businesses grow in this sad desert land. Ian that lost his only child and still gives the very shirt off his back to help someone. Ian, that wouldn't let me resign myself behind a crop insurance desk. *That* Ian has cancer.

Hat in my lap, I lean back against the seat and drag in a breath. Tears sting my eyes, and I swipe them as they fall.

Lord, how is this taking care of him? This doesn't feel like a good gift you're giving.

A little knock on the passenger window makes me sit up. Denise's straight hair falls around her face, and her eyes ask a gentle question. Leaning across the seat, I open the door and slide my leggins into the middle seat.

"You okay, sweetie?" Denise slips the question across the bench seat like a cozy blanket.

Another tear slides down my cheek. *Shouldn't I be the one asking her that?*

Her hand rests gently on my arm. "It's a lot to take in."

I nod and wipe at the tear trails on my cheeks. "Why him?"

How is it even humanly possible that a man bigger than life can be knocked down by a six letter word?

She nods. "Trying to figure out *why* will make you crazy." She scoots closer and puts her arm around me. The touch is all it takes to melt me. Head on her shoulder, the tears flow, and my chest shakes with breaths coming and going.

"It's going to be okay."

I nod against her shoulder. *It has to be.*

Denise rubs my arm until I sit up. Again I wipe under my eyes. I brush back the little hairs around my face and push my hat on my head. Looking to the house, a dread fills my stomach. A living nightmare.

I turn back to Denise and give her another light hug.

She bobs her head in the direction of the house. "He was at his desk." Her eyes are gentle but unwavering as they stare straight into mine.

I draw in a breath. Opening the pickup door, I will my legs to step out of the cab. She's right—I should go back in there.

I stuff my hands in my pockets and approach the wiggly-handled backdoor. Rustling around like an oversized rat in a feedsack reaches my ears when I'm just a couple feet inside the door. *Ian must still be at his desk.*

My mind scrambles for words to say. They're all wrong—all insensitive to the weight of the news.

The heels of my boots click on the floor. I peek around the corner to Ian at his desk with papers spread around him. I stall in the doorway not sure my voice will work. Stuffing my hands in my front pockets, I give it a try. "Busy?" I croak the word out.

He looks at me, a little startled for a second. "Trying to be." His hollow eyes go back to the papers.

"Looks like you're doing a pretty good job of it." I lean against the wall. "Looking for anything specific?"

He shakes his head, and a long exhausted breath leaves him. "Trying to make sense of all the options and research." He spins the chair away from the desk to face me.

Silence stuffs up the air around us. I shift my weight from one leg to the other. My feet want to walk, run, go anywhere. Just to keep moving.

I lick my lips. "Do you, uh, know what you do now?" I don't look at him, just enough in his direction to know his head is down.

"I won't do chemo."

That demands my gaze to focus on him.

He looks past me, and his hands bounce, forearms perched on his knees. "I've done some research on more natural treatments that have been pretty successful. I'll have to find someone around here that will do it."

My head moves up and down. I might need some banamine for colic later, because my gut is doing somersaults. "Will you go back to Midland for an appointment, or..." I don't finish. I don't know the alternative.

"They want me to next week."

I nod again; apparently, that's all my body can do. The silence gives my thoughts a chance to bounce through the most random topics. Only one is very related: I'm pretty sure I've been rubbing off on him, not quite actually answering the question and all.

The seconds tick by before his voice comes out a little raspy. "It's stage four."

Air catches in my chest again, just like when he said *cancer*. He looks at me, and I force myself to meet his eyes. "I'll be here wherever you have to go. I'll get the cattle tended to."

He's the one to break eye contact as he stands. Arm around my shoulders, he squeezes me in a hug. I put one arm around him and take my hat off with the other hand. My face presses into him, the snap on his shirt pocket just below my eye. I bite my bottom lip, not letting tears get any higher than the bottom of my throat.

"Thank you girl." His voice is soft and hitched with the tears he's not letting win either.

Chapter 7

The pallet of feed waiting for unloading makes my heart crumple up like a discarded piece of paper. Never thought I'd be in my twenties unloading feed for Ian because he didn't have the strength to, but here I am. Even yesterday's drive to town for a cake pickup was too much for him.

Mesquite leaves flutter in a breeze I can't feel as I step out of the feedroom door. I reach for another sack sitting on Ian's pickup and slide it to me.

The sack of feed flops onto the others already stacked on the pallet inside the feedroom. The thud stops echoing off the cement walls just in time for the ring of my phone to take its place. I pull it out of my pocket and read the name across the top.

James. My old co-worker.

For a couple of rings I just look at it. Then I click the button on the side, and it drops back in my pocket.

Talking is about the last thing I feel like doing right now.

Sweat drips off the wisps of hair that don't stay in the braid as I wipe more from the top of my lip. It soaks the cuff of my shirt. *It really shouldn't still be this hot.*

Another ten sacks are on the pallet when my phone rings again. I grit my teeth together. "James, take a freaking hint." Jerking it out of my pocket, I punch the decline button.

"I'm a little busy," I mumble under my breath, jerking the last sack off the pickup.

Mockingly, small talk plays in my head. My chest tightens, and I clench my fists. I can't handle a casual chit chat right now. I'll fall apart into more pieces than I can pick up.

Feed unloaded, I get the skid steer to put out hay. I rack my brain for why James would be calling me. Wade doesn't usually ship calves for another month, so that shouldn't be it. The clattering of the skid steer is obnoxious enough to keep breaking up my thoughts.

I wasn't at church this morning, but I've missed church before, and he hasn't blown up my phone. I shake my head. *Who knows.*

Cows fed, I step in the feedroom and wait for my eyes to adjust to the dim lighting. The all-stock feed I unloaded is in the corner. I guess that's what Ian feeds his horses, too. I pour from the open bag, finishing it off. The empty sack flutters into a pile with other ones, and I lug the five gallon bucket of feed outside.

My phone rings. Again. I pull it out of my pocket already sure I know who it is. Sure enough, the same five letters are displayed at the top of the screen.

James.

I slip through the gate with the bucket of feed. "Hello?" My voice comes out just as mouse-ish as I feel right now.

"Uh, hey." James's deep voice is halted. He must hear the same hesitation in mine.

Dadgummit, that's why I didn't answer all his other calls.

"Are you okay?"

I croak out a "yeah" and then let the pellets fall in the long metal trough. They drown out the dread I feel and the worry in his voice.

A long pause passes before he says, "You weren't at the sorting last night."

Halfway to the gate from the trough, I stop. He'd gone. All this time I've been trying to get him there, and he finally went. I want to laugh and be happy and ask him how it was, but I can't. There's nothing in my body that will put an ounce of effort into being happy.

"Missed you at church this morning too." He clears his throat. "And I went by your house to check on you." There's a little pause, and then he starts talking real fast. "I know I shouldn't have. You just weren't answering my texts either, and I got afraid Cante had pulled some dumb move and pinned you somewhere, but then he's up in the pens."

Tears have ahold of my throat now. They pool in my eyes and threaten to spill over. I swallow and look out across the horizon that's pink and blue and orange. "Ian's got cancer."

There. I said it. I said that hellish word out loud.

"Oh, Nor, I'm so sorry." The white static of a stiff wind fills the phone. "When'd they find out?"

I nudge a rock up out of the ground with the toe of my boot. "A week ago."

"What can I do?"

I shrug one shoulder even though he can't see me do it. I don't even know what *I* can do. Tending cattle and moving feed just doesn't feel like enough. "I don't know." My voice breaks on the end of the words.

"Is he going to do treatment in Midland?"

I shake my head. "I don't know." It comes out snappier than I meant, and I wince. "I'm sorry." I want to say that it came out of nowhere, but that's a lame excuse.

"It's okay."

I swallow. "It's stage four." *Terminal.*

"I'm sorry." His voice is barely a whisper, and the helplessness in his tone mirrors the feeling that hasn't left my chest.

Moments pass in silence. I roll the rock around under my foot.

"I'm going to come check on you tomorrow."

"James, no—"

"I didn't ask if I *can*." His tone makes that final. "I'll see you tomorrow."

"Thanks." I swallow and try to make my voice a little more cheery. "I appreciate it." As soon as I hit the red button, a sob escapes my chest.

I lean back against the gate post, hot tears starting to pave tracks down my cheeks. The crown on my hat presses into my head. I lean up long enough to turn the bucket over and sink onto it. Elbows on my knees, I drive the palm of my hand into my eyes. My chest shakes.

Ian being sick and going to the hospital was one thing. It was a short term kind of deal. At least it felt like it. But cancer? Anyone who's heard the word knows that it is a long haul.

I drag in a breath. He won't be on that haul by himself. Not if I have anything to do with it.

My rough knuckles slide under my eyes. *Crying here won't do anyone any good.*

I blow out hot air and will myself to my feet. I put the bucket away and close up the feed room. I make a circle by the dogs and check their water. A hand on the Chevy's door handle, I glance back at the house. Simple but strong. Just like the people inside of it.

"God, be with them." It comes out as a plea. Just one more day of waiting, and then maybe we'll have a game plan. I jerk the door handle, get in, and turn for my house.

It's nearly dark when I pull in there. I walk out to the pens and run a hand down the back of each of my geldings. They've been a bit more of a tool than a friend here lately. I drag them along when I need an extra set of feet, throw them feed once a day, and keep hay in the rack.

I wrap my arms around Banks's neck. "Y'all have always been there for me. Thanks boys."

After giving them each one more rub in their favorite spots, I pour them some feed. The pellets hit the trough with a ping. I let the sound die away and then step back through the gates and to the house.

I shower, lingering in the hot water. When I slip into an oversized shirt and shorts that barely stay on my hips, it feels like a stale hug. The sheets make it a little crisper still. I wrap them around me anyway and let the tears melt out of my eyes like water out of a slow deep well.

Chapter 8

Birds flitter around the mesquite tree by the pickup, tweeting cheer into the world that I can't muster an ounce of. Looking out at my geldings munching breakfast and swishing flies in the pens, I remember the exhaustion in Ian's eyes. I draw my knees up against my chest and lean back against the siding of my house.

I squeeze my eyes close, trying to erase the picture from my mind. The pain that haunts him. That stupid six letter word that hangs like a dark cloud over that whole place.

God... why?

I don't want to ask why, because He does all things for a reason, but I don't have anything else to say. It doesn't have to be like this, so why is it?

The idle of a diesel makes me wipe under my eyes and get to my feet. Not many people know how to get out here. But James does. My eyes close for a second and my lips lift just a little bit. He said he'd be out here today.

I step to the edge of the porch and watch the pickup roll to a stop. James's long frame unfolds from the driver's side. His hands find his pockets as his lips spread into a little bit of a smile.

He waits until he's an arm's length away from me before speaking. "How are you?"

Without warning, loud, bubbling sobs cave my chest in, and I cover my eyes with my hands. One arm wraps strongly around me, my hat leaves my head, and then there's the other arm holding me close to him. My body shakes with all the tears I haven't let fall today.

My sobs turn to dry gasps for air. It takes me several minutes to get my breathing controlled enough that I can talk. I lift my head from his chest and wipe under my eyes.

Gosh, I must look like a wreck. James has seen me get bucked off though. I guess this isn't much worse.

"I'm sorry." His voice is low and close to my ear.

I swallow. "It's okay. Just the biopsy they did has him so weak." My body gasps for another breath of air. "It's not supposed to be like this."

"No, it's not supposed to be like this." He smooths down my hair, and I find myself laying my head back on his chest.

After a moment, I lift my head, take my hat from him, and step back. "I'm sorry," I mumble.

"Don't apologize."

I look up at him. His eyes are much more serious than usual. *Man, I didn't mean to drag him down with me.* "You didn't have to come all the way out here."

His lips turn upward a touch. "Yes I did. I told you I was going to come check on you."

That he did. "Thanks."

His hands tuck in his front pockets. "What are you up to that I'm interrupting?"

"Just holding down the porch and avoiding checking waters."

The tone of his voice is just a little lighter than before. "Well, which one do you want help with? I've had practice with both."

Now I crack a grin, and one eyebrow raises. "You're going to go check waters with me? Don't you have enough work of your own?"

"I've got plenty, but I thought I'd try yours." He nods to the Chevy. "Is that what you are going to show me around in?"

Smiling, I shake my head. James always has been one of a kind. "Yeah, it is."

Before he can get in, I have to slip my leggins behind the seat and stuff a couple cans of grease under it. I start the engine, and he climbs in. The single cab isn't exactly suited for his long legs, but he's used to it. That's all Wade buys for ranch pickups.

Static plays softly through the speakers. I try to think of something to talk about, but I draw a blank.

"I got a dog." James blurts out. He props his elbow out the window.

I arch a brow. "Oh yeah? When did you do that?"

"Last month. Paid three hundred dollars for a brown catahoula dog. I thought that was going to kill me until they told me how much the leopard ones are. Found out I was getting off pretty good."

I chuckle with him. "Pup, then?"

"Yeah, he's nearly three months old."

James with a dog. *What a picture*. I never thought he'd do something so average. "I think a dog will suit you well."

I pull up next to the trough and hang my head out the window to inspect the water level. Looks good to me.

"They've still got one of his sisters…"

I idle the pickup away from the trough while staring pointedly at him. "No. I don't need another thing to keep up with."

His elbow nudges mine on the console. "Oh come on. She'll keep you from getting lonely."

I lean against the pickup door. "Nope." I pop the 'P' and then quietly add, "Of all the things, a dog is not what I need."

We bump along to the back of the pasture where the reservoir is. Before the wheels fully stop rolling, James reaches for the door handle. "I'll get it."

Okay then, I'll let you.

In a minute he jumps back in. "Good to go. It's about four inches low, but it's running."

"Thanks." It takes a moment before I convince myself to look over at him. I study his tanned face that wears a scratch under his check. One thought circles through my mind: he's bound to have more than enough work at home.

"What?" A stiff breeze makes him shove his hat firmly on his head.

Not quite daring to make eye contact, I watch the mesquite leaves wave out the window behind him. "I didn't mean for you to come over and work."

He waves dismissively. "I'm not about to come over and *watch* you work."

I narrow my eyes at him. *You could.*

"Just drive." He bumps my shoulder.

The pickup in first gear, I ease off the clutch and off we go. Again I'm trying to think of something to say, but I can't get past him caring so much about what I do or don't do. It's weird. No one's cared about my comings and goings that much since highschool.

Over a couple humps in the road and around another bend, I idle past another old sheep trough. It's full. My phone buzzes with a text from Mindi, but besides that the engine's purring is uninterrupted.

Just checking in on you. How's your family?

I click the screen off and put the phone in the cupholder. Falling apart doesn't seem like a very good answer to give.

It's a half mile or so down the road before James breaks the silence. "When are you going to let it rain?"

I scoff. "What makes you think I'm keeping it from doing so?"

A grin breaks out on his lips, and then he looks out the window. I lean over so my elbow bumps his hand that's stretched out on the back of the bench seat. My lips perk into a little smile, too.

By the time we get back to the house, I've nearly forgotten why he came over at all. Nearly.

He stands in front of my pickup and stuffs his hands in his pockets.

I chew on the inside of my cheek. "Thanks for coming over."

"Of course." His right hand leaves his pocket and cocks awkwardly in the air. "Let me know what you need. I mean that."

That's the second time he's told me he means it. *Man, it's like he knows me or something.*

James gets in his rig and heads for town. I step in the house for a quick drink as the purr of his pickup drifts away.

I've worked with James for years. And yet there's still a lot he doesn't know about me. Probably more I don't know about him. How have we gone all these years, hardly more than acquaintances?

I swallow the last of my glass of water and stare out the kitchen window at the settling dust.

And of all the times for things to change, it's now.

Chapter 9

Ian pushes the passenger seat back and sets his half-gallon water jug on the floorboard. "We'll be back Friday afternoon. We'll see how many holes they have to poke in my arm."

A grimace creases my chin and I'm thankful Ian's not looking. "Maybe they'll be able to leave an IV in and not re-poke you twice a day." I squint without my hat to shade my eyes. The big tree's shade doesn't quite reach this far at this hour.

A forced smile lifts one side of his lips. "I hope so." He puts his crisp black felt on the dash. "Take care of yourself."

I wrap my arms around him and stare holes into the duffle bags in the backseat. "Don't worry about things here. We'll be fine."

He lets go of me. "Thank you, girl."

I smile, a real one, before he folds himself in the passenger seat. "You're welcome."

Denise's door clicks, locking her in the driver's seat. I step back and let Ian pull his closed. The little engine starts purring, and then the wheels start turning. I lift my hand in a wave, fighting the nerves and pain in my gut.

The little red SUV disappears in a cloud of caliche. I bite the inside of my lip. The last time I watched them drive away like this was the start of the worst week of my life. This time it's supposed to be a good thing.

I pray that it is *the* thing. These vitamin C and alpha lipoic acid treatments *have* to work.

IN BETWEEN PASTURES

Feet heavy, as they have been a lot here lately, I trek to the old pickup by the saddle house. The handle pops as I jerk it. I hop in, and the cushion gives a little too much. *There's plenty of rods and pens holding this seat together.*

Cranking the window down as I bump over the cattle guard, I blow out a breath. Today is jam-packed, and there's already clouds hanging over my head. It should be a fun day.

My elbow hanging out the window gets smacked by a flying grasshopper. I tuck my arm back inside the door and switch to driving with my right hand. Half glazed over, I go through the motions for the first two troughs. Check the trough, look in the reservoir, note the salt and mineral for next time, jump back in the cab, and keep going.

The new tiger stripe cattle have made themselves right at home. Ian's Herefords in the back pasture are up at the trough when I pull up there. They rise as I walk to the cement tank. I rattle a half sack of feed on the bed of the pickup, sending the cows weaving out of the mesquites within a couple yards of me.

I'm about to string the cake out for them, but a hobbling calf makes me put the sack back on the pickup bed. Taking a closer look, I ease around the edge of the cows. He's young, probably a product of a bull jumping the fence. A pretty little red front leg with a white sock dangles right under the shoulder.

I run a hand over my face, grinding dirt into it. For a long moment I just stare at the little critter.

Chances are low he'll make it out here. It's too far between feed and water for him to have a leg hanging. My tongue turns dry in my mouth. Ian'll probably just say to put him down. I'd rather wrestle a breech out of a tiny heifer than go back to the house for a rifle and do that.

I blow out a breath and get back in the pickup cab. Maybe they'll follow me into the water lot. Don't know how I'll get a hold of him in there, but it's a start. At least they'll be easier to find.

A glance at the time makes me antsy. The list of things to do today is a mile long. But there's never a convenient time for a crisis, is there?

Easing off at turtle speed, I flip the switch and let the siren wail a couple times. The cows pick up a lopsided trot, creating a fan out from the bed of the pickup. I can't see the calf anymore, but I know he's going to be slower than cold molasses getting to the lot.

Fingers tapping on the top of the steering wheel, I ride the brake, keeping the pickup below five miles an hour. It doesn't even idle this slow. Every couple minutes, I blow the siren for a second, and the cows trot up a bit.

Just keep following, girls.

I poke my head out the window, but I still can't see the calf. Hopefully he's still poking along. A breeze blows, sending a shiver down my back where sweat has soaked my shirt from leaning against the seat.

The Gary Stewart cassette, that can barely be heard over the rattle of the engine, plays one side all the way through and half of the other side before I turn through the narrow gate of the water lot. While the cows mosey in at their leisure, *Empty Glass* and *Whiskey Trip* play. I toss one cube of cake out of the window at a time—just enough to entice them to come in and hang out.

When the dangly-legged calf finally straggles in, a weight lifts off my chest. I ease around the fence within a hundred yards of the gate. The cow who I think is the calf's momma is eyeballing it with twitchy ears. I take off in a mad dash. Dragging the wire gate across the gap, I get another good look at the leg. Poor thing might be better off if I did go get a rifle.

I'm too soft for that, though. They've got to have a fighting chance first.

The cows drift over to the far corner and start slowly milling. I pull my bottom lip between my teeth and judge how fast I can dash from the pickup to the wire gate. Not fast enough to turn that calf's momma back if they come in a hurry.

The cow I'm pretty certain is the calf's momma filters to the back of the group. If she'll stay there, I might get this done. I toss a few more cubes into the dirt before letting the wire down. I don't pull it back, just let it fall on the ground.

As I walk back up to the pickup, a couple cows split off and nervously trot a few yards toward the gate. I step in behind them but stay at a distance. Now would be a great time to acquire those eyes in the back of my head.

I take another step behind the two and then glance over my shoulder. Another cow wants to join them, but I can't tell if she's got the white spot on her neck making her the baby's momma or not, so I turn her back. As she does, she shows me her neck. It was not the momma.

"Dadgummit."

Three more start for the gate. While I'm squinting at the markings on their neck, another cow comes up the opposite fence. When I swing my head around, the first thing I see is that big white spot.

My heart starts running like it can get to the gate before my feet do. The feet that find a stick to stumble over, narrowly recover, and somehow keep up with the top half of my body. In my scramble to stay upright, I cause enough of a scene to turn the cow back.

For a few seconds, I hold onto the post and pant for oxygen. I can still feel my pounding heart thump against my chest as I ease back toward the pickup and the cows. A couple more filter out and take a wad of calves with them. The broke-legged calf is still up against the black brush bush he stopped under when he came in.

A cow and three calves I don't need eye me and then the gate, measuring the same thing I am. Who can make it there faster? A copper taste hits my tongue. I release the inside of my cheek from between my teeth before any more blood drips from it.

I'm *this* close. I don't want to lose the calf's momma. If I have to get her up horseback, it'll probably be with a rope.

The calf has hobbled over to a greasewood bush. I shake the dust off of the two ropes that hang above the spare tire. They should already be cut into pickin' strings, but they'll have to do.

I make a couple swings above my head with the more limber one and then feed more rope into the loop. It feels a little better then and I ease toward the calf. I swing two quick stiff circles around my hat and throw.

My face wrinkles in a cringe. The bottom of the loop is resting on the base of his neck, but the top is laid in the greasewood. I've caught more leaves than calf.

Slack held up in the air, I ease around until I'm just in front of the calf. Out of the corner of my eye, I see the cloud of dirt his momma is pawing up into the air.

"Stay over there bluffing, sister," I mumble. *At least I hope she's bluffing.*

My hands tense on the slack, waiting for the calf to jerk away from me. Three, four steps, and he still hasn't flinched.

I step over a black brush bush, cracking a branch. The calf jumps. My fist with the rope clasped in it slams against my hip, and the rope comes tight. My heart starts beating normal again and lets my lungs get back to work.

He's caught.

The little calf doesn't fight as I flip him on his side, bum leg up, and I tie his other three together. The bone wiggles around like it's in a bowl of half-set up jello. My spine crawls. That's got to feel awful. "I'm sorry, bud."

I stand and run a hand across my mouth, mind filtering through the list of possible splints. Two sticks straight and sturdy enough to make one are near impossible to find around here. There's not a mesquite big enough to produce one within a half a mile radius.

Shuffling over to the pickup, I pop a tool box open and start rifling through it. There's one five or six-inch long galvanized nipple.

That sounds like it'd be incredibly uncomfortable.

Up against one side of the tool box is a hack saw. I set it out on the flatbed. It might come in handy before I get this project done. On the other side of the pickup I pilfer some more. Some ratchet straps, bolt cutters, and a little piece of two-inch PVC pipe.

I pull the PVC out and squint at it. It's just long enough it might cover from the calf's shoulder to just below the knee. *Maybe*.

With the hack saw on the top of the pipe, I start cutting it into two long half circles. The name 'hack saw' fits very well with how those pieces turn out looking—like someone hacked them apart. They'll do the job, though.

After some more rummaging through the pickup, I tuck a half roll of duct tape under one arm and start back to the poor little critter. This is going to be one cowboy-rigged splint.

One half of the PVC on each side of the leg, I adjust the one on the outside to be up on the shoulder. Then I start wrapping it with slightly sunbaked duct tape. No telling how long it's been running around in Ian's pickup.

Two wraps up and down the leg from the shoulder to just below the knee uses just about the whole roll. I rub the end a bit so hopefully it stays stuck until I get back over here tomorrow.

I untie the pickin' string and stand the calf up on his feet. Momma stops throwing dirt in the corner and hums a low bawl. The calf doesn't even try to take a step.

Before Momma gets close enough that I have to worry about her throwing horns, I slip an arm under the calf's neck and one under his flank to tote him to the shade. At least he won't bake to a crisp while he waits for his momma to bring the lunch bucket.

I dump the three-quarters of a sack of cake beside the pickup and idle out of the lot. As I pull the make-shift hog panel gate closed, I glance at the shaded corner. Tripod hasn't gotten up, but the cow is licking her calf—and probably the duct tape.

Good Momma.

***

Idling the pickup under the tree outside Ian's house, I wilt against the seat. To the house—my house now—I go.

I slide my things over next to me in the seat before I get out. As I do, my phone starts vibrating in my back pocket. "Sheriff" reads across the top of the screen. I sigh and slide the green circle across. "Hello?" I don't even try to pep my voice up.

If the sheriff's calling, it's not good.

"Do you have cattle on 1676 about two miles off of 67?"

I slouch against the side of the pickup. "Yes sir."

"We had a driver run through the fence in the corner of your pasture here. There were a couple cows pretty close to this corner, but we scared them off."

Dust grates against my skin as I run a hand down my face. "Alright. I'll get over there in twenty minutes or so and fix it. Thanks for the call."

"Yes ma'am."

The phone lines beeps three times and that's that. I sigh. Never mind the burger I was thinking of grabbing on my way through town.

I drag my things from the passenger seat. Rolling my water jug into my pickup, I watch it tumble across the middle seat and bang against the door. I press my lips together. *Didn't want to drink out of that anyway.* After stuffing my pistol in between the cushions, I check Ian's pickup again and then slam the door.

Windows already down, the breeze starts whipping in as soon as the wheels cross the cattle guard. While I wait on a couple trucks to pass before getting on the black top, I lift the half gallon water jug and chug enough to make my stomach protest.

Just yesterday I took two t-posts and the t-post driver out of the bed of my pickup. They'd been rattling around back there for close to a month. Of course now that they're not here is when I could use them. I might not have to go by my house if they were still in here.

The tires growl. I make a mental list of the things I'll grab out of the barn. My stash of stay wire needs to be replenished, and there's a piece of barbed wire I need to throw in. Hopefully they haven't torn up too big of a stretch.

Once I've chunked the supplies in the pickup bed, I stop in front of my house and jog inside. The fridge door pops open easier than I was expecting and bangs against the counter. Dishes shift and clash together. I freeze with a cringe until I'm sure nothing is going to fall on the floor.

Eventually I'll get to the dishes. *Eventually.*

I grab a couple cheese sticks from the fridge and a half bag of tortilla chips off the counter, then I'm out the door again.

Mouth full, I look both ways before pulling out on the FM. I turn left and stay on the shoulder, only tootling along at fifty. A couple miles pass before there's black skid marks on the road. A few yards and then I see the laid over t-posts. Three of them.

Good grief, they did a number on this fence.

I drive past it a little ways and then lean up to watch the traffic. I whip across the road and into the bar ditch before the line of cars block me for a while. When the pickup bed is even with the mangled posts, I turn the ignition off and melt back against the seat. I stuff the last of a cheese stick in my mouth and crumple up the wrapper. My phone dings, and I flip it over. The whole screen is lined with notifications.

Most of them are variations of "See you tonight" in a group chat. My shoulders drop. *Horse club practice.*

How'd I forget? I rub a hand down my face. That's in just a few hours.

I clear a missed call from James, drop my phone in the passenger seat, and snatch the chips off the console. Before closing the door, I slide a pair of wire pliers in my back pocket. Bag of chips in hand, I survey the damage.

There'll be no resurrecting the t-posts, but the wire looks like it might be salvageable. At least a couple strands.

I leave my chips in the seat and grab a new t-post and the driver. I set it ten feet or so out from the closest standing one. Each pound of the metal driver smacking the post vibrates the insides of my head, making me desire a nap. I drive another one another ten feet down the fence line, though.

I get one existing strand of barbed wire unwound and tied up, but it sags. Somehow in my gathering of supplies the fence stretcher didn't make it in the pickup, so this'll have to do. The other three strands are toast. I guess we'll see if the piece I brought is long enough or not.

As I unroll it, a barb runs down the inside of my pointer finger. Just enough to split the skin and let a little drop of blood seep out. It stings a little.

Perfect. I drag it down my pant leg, leaving a tiny line of red, the cut stinging more than before. I give it a shake and grab onto the wire again. Before I get enough off the roll to reach the far post, the end pops loose. It zings past my head. I blink a few times.

I guess it doesn't need four stands of wire anyway. The poor cows are just hungry for half green grass like the bar ditch is full of.

Wire in hand, I lean back into the pull to stretch out some of the little coils. It barely gives it enough length to make a wrap around the t-post and then a couple loops back around itself. I step back and take in the sight.

A very slapped together sight at that. Like everything else I've gotten done today. Maybe it'll buy me the evening, anyway. I'll bring more wire over here in the morning.

Tossing the tools back in the pickup, I wipe sweat off my top lip. One more thing down.

The wind whips in the windows and dries any drop of sweat left. I glance at the time. It'll be a close one to get to horse club practice on time, but I should make it. As long as nothing falls apart between here and there.

Chapter 10

I push my door open with one hand and tug the key from the ignition with the other. There's already horses with half-grown kids on them loping around in and out of the arena. My strides eat up the distance between my pickup and the arena gate.

"Hey Daniel, sorry I'm late."

The forty-something dad and coach turns around and grins through his bushy beard. "No worries. We haven't gotten started yet." He nods towards the arena. "You've got some real go-getters in your group."

"They're doing great." I spot little Trace on his half-draft bay mare today instead of Mickey. He towers over a kid from Daniel's group.

A trailer rattles up, and by the time I pivot that direction, April's pulling herself up the side of Charlie with quite the determination on her face. She's a firecracker.

Daniel hollers at the kids to clear out the arena. While they filter out we set up barrels, putting a bucket of dirt with a flag sticking out of it on the top of one of them.

Slugging through the sand, Daniel's words are a little breathless when he says, "What do you do at your practices? I'm pretty sure I cheat at ours."

I look up from the red dirt. "We usually do some exercises for their horsemanship and riding ability and then focus on one playday event." I cover my yawn. "How about y'all's?"

"Oh, we go through the events a couple of times and then they play tag and some things like that. Much less learning-focused than what you do." He chuckles.

My chuckle matches his. "Probably more fun though." *My kids would probably prefer more fun.*

Before I have a chance to catch his reaction, a little sorrel horse with a not-so-little kid on top lopes into the arena. Daniel's head pops up just like my horses' when they see cattle running off. "Hey! Do you see anyone else in the arena?"

The kid draws up the reins and shakes his head.

"Alright then, maybe you shouldn't be either. Go warm up outside. We're about to get started."

"Yes sir." The kid turns his horse out of the arena at a trot.

"Kids." Daniel shakes his head, but I can't help the grin on my face. "So since we're doing this together, do we have a plan?"

My eyebrows raise. "I was hoping *you* did."

"I think we can make it through barrels and the flag race with each kid before it gets dark."

I look back over my shoulder at the horizon white with sunlight. *I certainly hope so.* "Sounds good."

Daniel's dad voice carries well as he hollers for the kids to gather around. "Alright, since we're sharing the arena between both practice groups, everyone will go through the flag race and then through the barrels. Five of you make a line to go first."

April directs Charlie around the outside of the group and rides up next to my perch on the fence. "Miss Nora?"

I turn halfway around, almost eye-level with her. "Yes ma'am?"

"I just got here, can I not go first?"

I nod. "Yes, go warm up some more."

"Thank you!" She calls it over her shoulder as she's already riding off.

A moment later there's a line of five horses outside the arena gate and a flashy little roan streaking toward the barrel with a flag on top.

I'm not really sure why they're here practicing if that's how they ride, but anyway.

He streaks back, making a circle in front of my perch on the fence. Once the roan has slowed to a prancing trot, the kid rides over and holds out the flag. Instead of taking it from him, I nod back at the barrel. "Can you take it back and stick it in the bucket?"

The boy looks at me a second and then nods once.

Thank goodness for horse feet. I'm too tired to traipse through the sand.

"Hmm," Daniel nods. "I like that."

I turn to him standing on the ground below me, and I guess the puzzle is clear on my face, because he lifts a hand toward the end of the arena.

"My legs get tired carrying it back to the bucket," he says.

Oh right, the flag. "Yeah, it's extra practice too."

The roan leaves the arena and is replaced by a big sorrel with a little kid on top. He's about as tall as Cante, and the thought makes me chuckle to myself. Maybe one day, when he's twenty, Cante'll be a kid horse like that.

Still on top of the fence, I shift to look over the kids riding around in the grass between the arena and the pickups. Daniel hollers something to the boy on the far end of the arena, capturing my attention for a moment. Focusing back on the field, I narrow my eyes at April and her gray horse. They've been fighting each other since they unloaded. I just thought he needed to warm up, but now I'm not so sure. He wrings his tail and does a little hop, popping her butt out of the saddle.

My eyes swell to saucers. She pulls her reins up, and the gelding's head levels out. I return to my slumped position on the top rail.

April's head spins my direction and her eyes find mine. That fear in her eyes makes the corners of my lips twitch. Mainly because I've been there too.

I raise a thumbs up, and her rein-hand lowers. Before turning back to the action in the arena, I make sure Charlie walks off like the little gentleman I've seen him be.

Kid after kid makes their round by the barrel with the flag on it. They get the flag and put it back—until we get to April. She walks Charlie up to the gate. "Miss Nora, is Charlie going to be okay with this?"

I climb off the fence to adjust her hand on her reins. "Just keep your hand down here to show him who's boss. You can do it."

She kicks him up into a trot. He takes a couple bumpy strides and I see her legs kicking, but he's not picking up speed. Then comes the tail slap.

I stand a little straighter and keep my eyes trained on the pair. "That's it, keep after him," I mumble.

April's legs go out in a kick determined to show him who's boss, and that's the very moment Charlie pops his rear-end up. I wince, my muscles freeze for an instance, and then my legs kick into overdrive.

April's little ten-year-old body flies over his right shoulder. The little *thunk* of her body hitting the ground sends my legs sprinting faster than I knew they could. Pea-sized dirt clods fly up with each stride.

April sits up just as I reach her, dirt smudging her nose and lips. No doubt she's eaten half a cup or more.

She seems more stunned than anything, so I raise my eyebrows, quirk a little smile, and hold up my hand for a high five. "Nice ride, cowgirl." *It's a whole lot easier to get back on when no one makes it out to be a big deal. I've had plenty of experience.*

She gives me a half-hearted high five.

"Do your toes still work?"

Eyes trained on her feet, she nods.

I give her a hand to stand up and then put that hand on her shoulder. Propping my hat back so that I can see her eyes, I make my voice real soft. "What about your voice?"

Heavy steps sound behind me. April looks past me and then nods. "Yeah, I'm okay." Her voice wobbles like tears might follow it. She starts to brush the dirt from her clothes, so I dust the back of her.

"Let's get you some water to wash that dirt out of your mouth." I extend my hand, and only after her smaller one fits in it do I look up.

Daniel approaches with Charlie in hand. "You alright?"

April's head wobbles in a nod.

I give him a pressed smile before glaring at the horse. "Will you just hang on to Charlie for me for a sec?"

He nods, and if I'm not mistaken there's a little smug grin he's holding back. "Yes ma'am. There's waters in the ice chest in my truck."

"Thank you."

The more my feet sink into deep-tilled dirt, the more deep-set anger bubbles inside me. *That dang horse.* Six months ago when I first met April she wouldn't ride on her own. Just the last couple months has she decided loping is okay. Now this!

I retrieve a water from Daniel's cooler and take the lid off. "Take a drink of that and swish it around."

As she spits it out, April's dad Joe walks up. He smiles at me with raised eyebrows and then rumples his daughter's already crazy hair. "You didn't tell me you were going to be a bronc rider."

I look down at April, my muscles not so bound up now. At least her dad is calm about it. The plastic bottle in her hand shakes just a little bit. "Are you okay to stay here with your dad?"

She looks up at me. "Yes ma'am, I'm okay."

"Good. I'll be back in a few minutes." I give her a big grin but let it drop the moment my back is turned to her.

My portable tack room I've been toting around in my pickup seat just got unloaded yesterday, or I'd have my boots and spurs. Might be better that I don't though. Tennis shoes do less damage. *But they'll get less attention out of him.*

At the arena gate, Daniel hands me the gray's reins. That smug grin is in fact on his face. I cock my lips to one side in a reply of sorts. Daniel's been around one too many cranky horses like Charlie too.

I let the near side stirrup out to the last hole. Without asking, Daniel does the other side and then nods once at me. "All set."

"Thanks." I slip a rein on each side of the gelding's neck and get on. My knees nearly touch the swells, they're so wadded up. I'm pretty sure half my butt is on the cantle itself. I settle myself in the saddle as well as I can and then smooch Charlie off.

I let him have a few strides before I smooch him again. His tail whaps against his butt. My eyebrows arch. *Alright then buddy. You're not the only one who knows how to play that game.*

The pickin string I'd tied to the swell of April's saddle several weeks ago is still there. I untie it and slap it against my leg. It stings, but the gelding throws his head a little, so I do it again. It does nothing for his attitude, so he gets it smacked against his butt.

I feel him coil up to kick and I cringe. These jockey stirrups aren't going to be great for that. He doesn't though, instead giving me a stiff lope.

That's better.

We make it to the end of the arena, in a circle and then I tap him with my heels.

Dang, it feels weird not to have spurs.

The little gray coils up again, and this time I don't give him a second chance. I lay the rope string against his butt once and then again. He double barrel kicks.

My torso jolts forward, hands fishing around in front of me for that little bitty saddle horn that's supposed to be there somewhere.

Knees clamped against his sides, I latch onto the pickin' string again and raise it. As soon as Charlie sees it in the air, he grabs a gear.

In a blind mad run, the gray whizzes down the fence, around the end, and halfway up the other side of the arena. Finally he starts to slow. I let him drop to a normal lope but give his sides a good tap to keep him at that pace.

Back at the end by Daniel and the kids, I turn Charlie to the barrel pattern. On my way by the third barrel, I reach over for the flag. I feel the wooden dowel stick graze against my fingertips but we whiz by it.

Charlie is happy to slow down when I lift the reins as we come up on the gate. His sides heave with each breath.

"Not quite so frisky," Daniel comments as he opens the gate for us.

I crack a smile as we ride through. *Not quite so opinionated now that's for sure.* I walk Charlie past the crowd of kids and into the grassy patch. After a couple quiet circles at a trot, I pull him up and step to the ground. My right knee screams at me, and I grit my teeth.

April's face is cleaned up with only a few dirt spots left. Her hand is still wrapped around what I'm pretty sure is the same water bottle.

I put on a bright smile for her and hold out one of the reins. "I think we got his attitude adjusted back to where it should be."

Only after a little nudge from her dad does she reach for the leather. "Do I have to get back on him?"

A three letter word—yes—tries to tumble off my tongue, but I look up at her dad first. Joe nods once. A silent man he is. Like Ian.

Suddenly the red car disappearing in a cloud of caliche dust appears in my mind—I swallow. *Focus*.

"Just ride at a walk." I glance up at the other end of the arena. "How about we take him down to the round pen and you ride him there?"

She shakes her head.

Joe squats down and props his cap back on his head a little. "Sweetheart, you can't let Charlie get away with that. You don't have to go fast, just walk him."

The softest "okay" leaves the little girl's mouth.

I glare at the horse, even as April's dad helps her to her feet. She was building so much confidence. Now we'll have to start over on that.

Joe tells her something in a low tone, and then she leads her gelding away. "What do you think is his deal today?"

I stub at a rock. "He was trying to be a bit of a pain last time. I think he's just getting a little sour attitude."

"Thank you for taking care of her."

I shrug one shoulder. "Of course." It's not like I did anything special.

He walks off to catch up with his daughter, and I turn back to the arena with a yawn.

"Nora."

I turn to the sound of my name, blinking away the moisture the yawn drew to my eyes. When they focus, I see Mindi walking my way with her lit up phone in her hand. "Hey, how are you?"

She takes cheater glasses off her nose and dazzles a row of white teeth. "I'm doing good." The tip of her glasses shifts to me. "How's your uncle doing?"

My chest grabs itself like a colt and I roll a rock under my boot. "He's hanging in there. They're starting some IV Vitamin C and other IV treatments this week."

"Glad to hear that." She taps her phone screen. "I've been visiting with a couple people. Joe and Daniel are going to take over your kids' practices for a little while."

My eyebrows pop up. I hadn't thought much about stepping back. But with everything that's fallen apart in less than twenty-four hours since Ian rolled out of the driveway, it's not a bad idea. "Are you sure? I can swing it."

Her hand rests on my shoulder, commanding my attention. "You've got enough on your plate. Let us help this way."

My throat's choked up, so I just nod. *The idea of a freed up Sunday evening to check in on Ian and Denise does sound lovely.*

Chapter 11

The thud of my pickup door is music to my ears. I turn the key and flip my phone face up on the seat to read the time.

8:59

I must be getting old. It feels much later, and I didn't even have that early of a morning. I contemplate going by the hole in the fence from earlier but decide against it. Aside from going to the house and getting more stuff, there's nothing I can do for it. Once I get to the house, something'll have to be on fire before I'm leaving it.

Putting the Chevy in gear, I scrunch up my face. Why'd I even think that? The way things have been going lately it'll probably end up happening.

Please, God, nothing else tonight. I pull out onto the highway. *Maybe for a few nights.*

The Chevy's wheels stop turning in front of the house. The front door has never looked so welcoming, its chipping paint and all. I grab my pistol from between the seat cushions and the empty water jug from the floorboard. Feet on the ground, it feels like I'm loaded down with sandbags.

I plop the items on the kitchen table and head to my bedroom. *Shower and bed.* The three words roll over and over in my head like a chant. A shower and then to bed. That's all I have to do.

The dresser drawer squeaks open, and in a fraction of a second all hope of a shower and bed drains from my body. There are no tee shirts. There are no shorts. No pajamas.

I rub my cheeks with cracked, callused hands. I spilled creamed coffee down the front of my last clean pjs this morning. The rate this day is going, I won't have skin left there for me to run my hands down.

I lug the dirty clothes hamper to the washer by the back door. Not paying attention to what's what, I drag half of it into the washer, drizzle some soap on top, and hit start.

The few steps back into the kitchen are more sluggish than the ones through arena sand. I sink into a chair at the table. A roll of my neck pulls on muscles down my shoulders. They'll just have to stay tight. There's no gumption left for massaging the knots out of them.

Staring at the fountain of dishes in the sink, I zone out. The washer's groans change pitches bringing back a little bit of my focus, and I push myself from the chair. The fridge door comes open with a sticky pop. I'll just add that to my list of things to do. *Clean the fridge.*

A half jug of tea, a crockpot with at least a handful of beans, and a block of cheese that was once five pounds, are all that sit on the shelves. There's butter and ketchup in the door. All that together in one pot sounds disgusting.

I pull out the beans and cheese, place them on the counter, and turn to the cabinet that serves as a pantry. The chips I ate earlier were the last of them. Poking around behind a stack of tuna cans, I uncover a few crackers left in a sleeve.

Beans fished out of the crockpot, I add cheese to the skillet and stir. By the time my arm's tired of making circles, the cheese is only half melted. I tap the spoon on the side of the skillet and lay it on the counter.

To heck with keeping it from sticking.

I turn the burner down just a hair above killing the fire completely and then sink back into my chair. My eyes won't hold open very much longer.

They must stay drooped for a few minutes, because next thing I know the skillet's contents are bubbling. Jumping up, I flip the burner off and slide the skillet to the back of the stove. Fishing around in the drawer beside the stove, I find a couple potholders. I take the skillet to the table, first plopping a potholder down.

Over the smooshing of crackers in my ear I hear my phone ding. I scan the table for it, but when I don't see it, I look over my shoulder on the kitchen counter. I stuff another cracker in my mouth and chew it up before pushing myself to my feet.

Waiting on the little screen is a message from James.

How are you doing?

I sink back into the kitchen chair and lift a spoon full of cheesy goodness to my mouth. I hesitate. How much do I tell him? Typing with one hand, I keep it short.

Tired. It was a long day.

Moments later it dings again. *What happened?*

Ian left for treatment. Set a calf's leg. Fence got ran through. Kid practice was a mess... yeah. I smoosh another cracker between my teeth.

How much fence did they tear up?

Not too much. It could have been worse.

That's good.

A couple seconds pass and then another gray bubble pops up.

Are you doing okay with Ian's stuff?

I've no more than read the first one when another pops up.

I mean, I know it's hard.

I grasp the phone tighter, thumbs hovering over the keypad. Squinting, I read his messages again. *It sucks.* I erase that and stare at the keyboard. *Kinda went numb today. I just try to take care of everything so he doesn't have to worry over it. I can't think about it or else I won't get anything done.*

I hit send before I erase that too. Then I click the screen off and pull the skillet closer.

I shove a spoonful in my mouth. Tears start climbing their way up my throat, gripping it with their suffocating hands. The cheese in my mouth turns into a wad of rubber. I lay the spoon against the cast iron and shove it away.

I manage to get the food swallowed past the tears. My arms feel limp. Leaving the half-full skillet on the table, I grab a towel from a laundry basket in my bedroom and go straight for the bathroom. I turn the hot water on and let it run while I peel my sweat stained clothes off. By the time I step in, the water is scalding.

The water and sweat residue masks the salty tears rolling down my face. I let them.

When I finally step out, my hair is dripping, and I feel a little more human. I wrap myself in the towel and pad out to snag another one for my hair. The washer isn't groaning anymore. I move its contents over to the dryer and slink back into my bedroom even though there's no one around to see me.

Perching on the little sliver of bathroom counter, I fiddle with a stray hair tie. If only I could snap my fingers and put everything back the way it was a couple weeks ago.

A couple weeks. That's all that it's been. I lean my head back against the wall. The longest fourteen days of my life. Even longer than the half month before I moved off of Wade's place.

Like a highlight reel, images swirl through my mind. *Wet Hereford calves, groups of the bald face cattle racing each other, and the half-grown heifers throwing their tails in the air in early morning air.* I wrap my arms around myself. Something about those days spread a blanket of warmth over my heart.

That day Ian came over to help me pull a breech calf. My lips press a smile into a thin line.

Bittersweet.

When the dryer buzzes, it jolts me from my daydream. I shuffle to the machine and pull a couple pieces of clothes from it. They're damp, but warm.

In an oversized t-shirt and a pair of shorts, I flip off the kitchen light. The stove clock reads 12:05. Taking my phone from the table, I head for the bedroom and slip under the covers. After a couple seconds, I lift the phone and click the button on the side. The screen lights up with a message.

It's okay not to know how to feel about it. But you don't have to do it all alone, Nor.

Chapter 12

Pant legs dragging against the hardwood floors, I shuffle over with my mug and pour it to the brim with steaming coffee. I take it to my brown chair and draw my legs up onto the cushion with me. Laying my head back, I let my eyes flutter close.

Before my eyes can stay that way too long, I lift my coffee cup to my lips and take a sip. And then another. I've about talked myself into putting some boots on when the quiet of the morning gets jarred loose by the ringing of my phone.

In a little faster shuffle than before, I make it to the kitchen before it stops its racket. "Hello?"

"Hey girl."

My shoulders relax in a droop at the thread of strength in Ian's voice. I sink into the nearest chair. "How's it going up there in the big city?"

"Ah, it's pretty boring up here. That's why I called you. How are things down there?"

I pick at a stray string on my jeans. *Not boring.* "Well, I patched up a broken leg on a calf yesterday." I wince as soon as the words ooze out of my mouth. He doesn't need another thing to worry about.

"Up there at Clay's?"

My mouth goes dry. "No, one of your little hereford calves."

"Well darn." There's a second's pause where if I was sitting across the kitchen table from him, he would pick up a toothpick and turn it between two fingers. "You think it'll make it?"

"He's not much over a week old. Still got a good chance it'll grow back together. I have him a splint of PVC and duct tape right now." I lift my coffee for a sip.

"Good." There's a pause. "What else is going on?"

I swallow. *My world is falling apart?* I shake my head. Not half as bad as his world has fallen apart. "I got to train on a kid horse last night at horse club practice."

While I recount my fight with Charlie, I find my favorite loafing shoes, refill my coffee, and head for the pens. I peek over the fence to check the horses water and try to direct the conversation away from me. "What do they have you up to today?"

"Just holding this chair down at the clinic for the morning. I've been watching John Wayne and napping at the rental house in the afternoons."

Another sip of coffee. "Sounds like you're living it up."

"Something like that." There's some muffled talking through the phone line. "I've got to let them have this arm and the other one is already tied up. I'll holler at you later, girl."

"Alright, don't have too much fun."

A slow breath seeps out between my half parted lips. So many half finished words and thoughts scramble in my brain. I ache for the days when I'd drive up to Ian's house, or office, and have nothing to worry about other than when it will rain and the latest story we can drag up from the past to swap with each other.

I just want those days back.

I set my coffee cup on a turned over bucket in the saddle house and grab a halter. A sprinkling of feed in the trough brings the horses from their stake just outside the pen. I close the gate behind them before hemming Dune up in the corner and tying the rope halter on him.

He's had enough work lately that he ought to be on the ground enough to pick Tripod the calf up on.

Leading him over to the saddle house door, I wrestle with the cloud of thoughts hanging over my head. I didn't even ask Ian how treatments were going. He didn't offer, but I darn sure didn't press. How am I supposed to support him through this if I can't even ask him how he's doing? He's done so much for me. What if he's fading away in the rent house in town and I don't even know about it?

The trilling ring of my phone draws me out of my trance. I lift it from my shirt pocket and read the name across the top. James. Our texts circle through my mind.

I'm numb... so he doesn't have to worry... you don't have to do it alone.

I silence the ringer, then I toss the device on a stack of feed and pull my saddle from its peg.

I can spill my guts over a text message to James, but I can't even ask Ian if he's doing alright. I shake my head and swing the saddle up onto my five-year-old gelding's back. That's not how it's going to be anymore.

The cinch buckles clink together as I drop them on the off side of the saddle. I'm not sure how I'm going to get my crap together, but I have to. I have to patch myself together enough to be there for Ian right now.

When I reach the water lot, the three Herefords throw their heads up. It takes a couple scans of the little lot before I pick Tripod out, standing by himself behind a greasewood bush. The duct tape splint is gone.

Of course it is.

Before I bother them any further, I go ahead and back the trailer up at an angle to the only real gate out of the trap. The trailer gate latch squeals, stirring Dune from his nap. He backs out at a snail's pace. Then I wrap his reins around a t-post and tie the trailer gate open. It's a slim chance this will work, but I'd rather try than coax that cow into following me with her calf slung over the front of my saddle. That sounds like a recipe for disaster.

On Dune, I start easing around the lot, partly watching the cows for a good chance to cut the extra off, partly watching the ground for the PVC splint parts.

I find the splint first, still halfway held together with crinkled-up duct tape. I retrieve it and toss it over the fence by the trailer.

Hopefully I remember to pick that up.

When I've ridden up within a couple feet of Tripod, I start to get off and catch him, but he must know what's up. He trots off at a good little speed for carrying a leg. I ride a short ways out from him and in front before I dismount. Stalking a few steps closer, I rush in for a grab. Going for his neck, I end up with my arms wrapped around his flank. He pops his butt up, slamming right into the side of my face. My teeth rattle and clamp around a piece of my cheek. It tingles. Wincing and spitting, I clamp my arms around him a little tighter.

IN BETWEEN PASTURES

I reposition with an arm around his neck and one under his flank to tote him over to Dune for a string off my saddle. The sorrel rocks back on his hindquarters and snorts a little. "Whoa," I say under my breath, then spit out a wad of blood.

String in hand, I lay Tripod over on his side and tie his three good legs together. Then hoisting him up again, I carry him up into the front of the trailer. I start to lay him on the wooden floor boards, but don't want him getting crushed. With a grunt, I wrestle him up into the nose of the trailer. "Good decoy." I pat him on the top of the head.

From a piece of a sack of cake, I pour a little pile halfway up the trailer. *Between cake and her baby, surely Momma will get in.* I sure hope so, because I'm fresh out of ideas otherwise.

Dune has worked his way up to the trailer, stepping on his reins about every other footfall. I gather up the two pieces of leather, jump to catch the stirrup with the toe of my boot, and swing my leg over. Cupping my hand over my mouth and flapping it back and forth, I make my best impression of a calf. The cows' ears flick forward.

Good girls, go check it out.

I direct Dune around the fence at an easy walk until we are behind them. They've taken a few steps towards the trailer. In a few more they start working their nose, lifting their heads to get a better whiff of cake.

There you go, go on.

My breaths grow shallow as they take a few more steps. Maybe it's going to work. *Maybe.*

A few minutes pass, and then there's a hoof in the trailer. Another and another until one cow is all the way in the trailer rolling a piece of cake around. I crane my neck to see which one it is, but I can't see the markings well enough to know. Probably the extra, just because they can be that kind of complicated.

I itch to step Dune up and put a little pressure on them, but I sit back in the saddle. *Slow's fast.* The seconds tick by. I swallow and adjust my hand on the reins. The trailer floor boards creak. I lean up in the saddle a little.

There you go sister. Get in there with her.

Another hoof, and then the last. I spur Dune, and he lunges forward. The cows crowd to the front of the trailer. I wince but bail off and pull at the string holding the trailer gate back. *Don't crush Tripod up there.* The gate slams and then I push the latch around.

My mind races ninety miles an hour, and my feet try to keep up. I jump up on the fender of the trailer and walk to the front. The cows crowd to the back, and I push the partition gate half closed. One cow slips through, and I slam the gate closed before I even know which one it is.

Crouching down to look through the bars of the trailer, I see Tripod's momma's big marking on the side of her face.

"Yes!" I drag the word out with a hiss and smile wide enough it splits my chapped lips. It's rare I get the right one on the right side the first time.

I kick the extra cow out of the trailer and hop back on Dune. He carries me over to the wire gate in the opposite corner, and I lay it open so the cow can rejoin her friends in the pasture.

Dune steps up into the back half of the trailer, and I close him in. I thread the pickin' string holding the gate back through the rungs of the trailer and pull it tight. Stepping away from the trailer, my toe stubs the PVC pieces.

Oh, right. I lean over and fetch the pieces I'd already forgotten about.

Pulling away from the lot, I look at the time. Only thirty minutes to do all that. *Not too bad. Not too bad at all.*

At Ian's pens I make the circle drive to line the trailer up with the alley. I lean up and crane my neck, but I still can't tell how close I might be. I ease off the brake, the tires starting to roll, and then the bump of trailer against pipe answers that for me. *There it is.*

My phone buzzes with a text. I reach over for the two rolls of vet wrap in the passenger seat before I open the message from Mom.

Hey, we're on our way back from seeing Ian and were going to swing by. Will you be at home?

I squeeze the roll of vet wrap between my fingers. *Thanks for the heads up y'all were going to be anywhere in the country today.*

Yes, I will. I type out directions to get to my house and hit send.

I push open the pickup door and grab the two pieces of the make-shift splint. Both of them fit in one back pocket of my jeans. A roll of vet wrap takes up the other, and I slide the second roll in my shirt pocket.

My spurs jingle with each step down the side of the trailer. If Mom and Dad really are just leaving Ian's rent house, it's just over an hour before they're at mine. I better get little Tripod tended to pretty quick.

My day never goes the way I plan it. I guess their visit is better than something being torn up, though.

I back Dune out of the trailer and loop his reins over the fence outside the alley. Before I open the partition gate to let the cow out, I set the pens up to shoot her back to the bale of hay. As soon as the trailer's middle gate shows a couple inches of room between it and the side, the cow lowers her head and pushes it the rest of the way. It slams back against the trailer with a bang.

That's one way to do it.

I close the gate out of the alley behind her and then tote the little guy out of the trailer. There in the alley, I lay Tripod over on his side and wrap the PVC pieces on either side of his leg. The poor little guy doesn't even offer a fight.

I stand back and observe his new wrap. *Not too shabby.*

I scoop him up again and carry him into the pen with the hay. As soon as I pull back, he takes a couple hobbled steps toward his momma. I nod, as if that will do something for him, and watch him take several more before leaving the pen.

After dumping a half sack of feed out for them, I jump in the pickup and high tail it out of there. I'll be cutting it close to make it to the house before Mom and Dad do.

The highway is pretty clear, so I run eighty-five with the rest of the law-breaking citizens until I turn on the county road. There's too many holes and dips to go even fifty on it.

IN BETWEEN PASTURES

Pulling up to the house in a cloud of dust, the first thing I see is Mom's head poked inside the backseat of their half-ton Ford. It pops right out as soon as I park in my usual spot beside the house. I drag in a deep breath, slap on a smile, and beg the emotions in my throat to go away.

Daddy is standing at the end of the pickup, surveying the pens. I open my mouth, but words get caught in the back of my throat. I stuff my hands in my pockets, but before I can try again, he turns with his wide, observing eyes.

"Looks like they've got you a pretty nice set of pens."

Glancing out at the pens, I raise my eyebrows. *That's one thing to think about right now.* I meet the one-armed hug he extends to me and let myself lean against him for just a second. "They're a little funky to work cows in, but all the gates swing."

His eyes connect with mine in a stare deep enough to count the veins in my heart. I look away.

How was Ian? What made you decide to come down? Have y'all gotten any rain lately? But none of those things come out of my mouth. I just move a rock with my boot and stuff my hands in my pockets.

"Hey! There you are." Mom throws her arms, one of them with a Walmart bag hanging off of it, around me. But the hug is stiff and awkward.

When I'm released, I nod to the bag. "What you got there?"

"Sandwich fixings fit for a queen." Daddy shakes his head, an amused smile parting his lips. "Your mother has gone to great lengths to make sure that while she may be delivering sandwiches, it's the best one you've ever had."

I chuckle. "Well, have y'all already eaten some of them, or would you like to join me?"

"We ate with Ian and Denise." The Walmart bag hisses as Mom clenches it tighter.

Dad's sideways glance doesn't go unnoticed. I didn't know the air could get this tense standing outside. Learn something new everyday.

I scan the rocks for the particularly round one I've been pushing around. "How bad does he look?"

"He's hanging in there. Has a good attitude about it all."

I glance up at Dad. *That wasn't the question I asked.* His answer gives my imagination enough to run with, though.

In a moment, Mom's looking me up and down. "Honey, you haven't been skipping meals again, have you? You need to make sure you're taking care of yourself." Her voice is airy, but her words are serrated.

Here we go again. Doesn't matter what I do, it's not enough.

I start for the house. "I'm feeding myself just fine, Mom."

"How are you doing taking care of both places down here?" My father's voice holds an edge. I'm not sure if it's about what Mom said or the fact that he doesn't think I'm capable.

Either way, my spine straightens, and I have to bite the inside of my cheek. I push the door in and talk over the groan of the hinges. "It's going alright. Everything's staying afloat so far."

So far might be the key words in that statement, but he doesn't need to know that.

Dad nods. "Good, good. Ian's lucky to have you."

No, I'm lucky to have him.

Mom's no more than two feet into the house before she starts fixing. The sandwich things are dropped on the bar, and she bee-lines it for the sink. "Oh, honey, do you have any plates clean?" She rips off a couple paper towels. "That's okay, you fix you a sandwich on here and I'll get on these dishes."

"It's okay, Mom. I'll get them later." I take the paper towel anyway. At the mention of food, my belly has started telling me about it. "Come catch me up on the happenings at home."

"Is this a mixing bowl?" Mom stops long enough to look over her shoulder at me. "You've been baking? I'm so proud of you."

My dad perches on a bar stool and shakes his head. "It's no use," he mumbles lowly.

It never has been any use to tell either one of you anything.

I stuff my sandwich in my mouth before words I regret spill out. It's an exceptional sandwich. So at least Dad is right about something.

Chapter 13

The cracked white paint covering Ian's house stares me down. The pickup door seems to weigh three times as much as usual as I heave it open. These first weeks of treatment have been rough on Ian. I have to prepare myself to go in and face that. Out in the pasture, I can pretend he's just at his office swamped with clients. Once I step inside, I'll have to face the truth.

Just before I reach the back door, I run into Denise coming around the end of the house. I lick the dust off my lips. "Afternoon." Thankfully my voice comes out light enough.

"Hey, Nora. He's asleep. I decided I'd get out of the house so I don't wake him up."

I put my hands in my pockets. "It's a pretty nice day to be out here." Considering we're into June already, we better take it while we can get it.

"It is." Her fingers stroke a plant that's perched on a stand by the door. "I'm sorry we didn't get to the waters this weekend. It's been a rough few days."

My gut churns. "I guess that's probably pretty normal—for it to come and go." I try to leave a question mark at the end of that. I couldn't write a paragraph on what I know about cancer.

"Yeah." She blows out a breath. "That's what the nurses say at the clinic. These treatments give his body what it needs to fight it. Sometimes it seems like it's everything he needs, and sometimes it's not."

There's a lump in my throat that won't swallow away. All I can think to do is pray, but the only word I can manage is a desperate heart cry of "Lord". I put my hand on Denise's shoulder. She looks up at me with tears hanging in her eyes, and we wrap our arms around each other.

Denise pulls back and wipes her cheeks. "Ladies from church have been bringing meals by the rental in town every few days." A smile fights against the sadness downcasting her face. "They've even stuck to the food guidelines Ian's supposed to be on since starting these treatments."

The breath I take in comes easier than I expect. *At least they aren't completely alone up there during the week.*

"Thank you again for taking care of things here. We appreciate it."

Pressing my lips together in that little straight lined smile I've been using a lot these days, I weave my fingers together. "Of course. Is there anything else I can do today?"

Her gaze drops back to the plant. "Not that I can think of."

I start to turn away then stop mid-stride. The words in my head get hung up in my mouth, making me swallow before trying again. "How are things at his office? Is there anything I can do to help there?"

Denise shakes her head. "I've taken care of a lot of the paperwork for a while, so it's nothing new. He only has a few clients he's buying or selling for, and Owen Hicks has been taking care of that." She dusts her hands against each other. "So far he's been able to keep up with it, just slower than usual."

"Owen as in Mr. Wellman's son?"

Denise nods. "Wellman got him on it as soon as he knew about Ian's diagnosis."

"That sounds like him." I tuck my hands inside my front pockets and look at the house. Ian needs all the rest he can get. He doesn't need me barging in and waking him up.

I shuffle my feet. "I'll come by after church tomorrow and tend to things."

"Tell them we appreciate the prayers." Denise lifts a hand and touches my arm lightly. "And if it's just the horses, I can take care of that."

"Alright. I'll be by Monday then." I turn back to my pickup by the barn before more feelings manifest on my face. There's a battle every day. I don't want to come over at all because then I might have to accept what it's reduced his body to. At the same time I want to lay eyes on him everyday and know I'm doing something that's helping.

The Chevy stops under its tree at my house, and I glance at the time. Five o'clock. I run my hand down my face before pushing the door open. If life was normal I'd be headed to practice with the horse club kiddos.

I sink into my comfy chair and pull a basket of laundry up beside it. My shoulders droop, and I lean back into the cushion. Honestly, I'm kinda glad Mindi got practice covered. It feels good not to be rushing on to something else.

I've just dragged up another bath towel to fold when my phone starts ringing in my pocket. *James.* I listen to its chime as I stare at the screen. My finger itches to touch the green circle, but my heart recoils when the text I sent him replays in my mind.

And all I'd told Ian was a brush off. The phone rings several more times before I hesitantly tap the green circle and lift it to my ear.

"Hey."

"Hey, your phone does still work."

Guilt lodges hard in my stomach as I lay the folded towel on the arm of the chair. "Yeah," I mumble.

"Busy day?"

I pry myself out of the cushions and take the stack of towels under my forearm. Letting out a long breath, I try to recall when the day even started. "Yeah, I guess so."

"I hardly ever see you in town, so I figured you've been keeping yourself that way."

I laugh a little. "James, you didn't see me in town before..." I swallow a sudden copper taste in my mouth as the words I was about to say die away.

The bathroom cabinet door swings back against the wall. I swallow and take in a couple breaths. There's a long moment of silence. I slip the towels into their place.

His voice is low and gentle when he says, "Could I talk you into taking a little break from running around all over the country?"

My thumb nail hits a tender spot under my ring finger, and I wince. I'm glad to be back at the laundry to give my hands something to do.

"How about I take you to dinner this week?"

My breath gets caught in my throat. Dinner? With him? That's a recipe for spilling my guts again. "James, I can't—"

"Nor, just some Mexican food and maybe a laugh. Just to relax for one whole hour."

I want to laugh *now,* only my chest won't move. Does he know how much I don't relax going out to eat with people? At the same time, it does sound nice to *not* shove food in my mouth at record speed while trying to wash dishes or check waters.

"Okay." The word slips out, but instead of making it harder to breathe, my chest relaxes.

"Great!" I can hear the grin on his face. "What day? I'll see if I can fit it into my busy social life."

I stack another bath towel and steady the pile. *He's impossible.* "Sunday? Clay doesn't like me slaving away on Sunday anyway."

"Good. I'll pick you up at six tomorrow."

My heart wads up like Cante when he gets spooked. Right. Tomorrow *is* Sunday. "You don't have to—" I don't get to finish my half-baked thought.

"I'm picking you up."

I sigh, my chest having relaxed just a little. "Six, then."

"I'll see you then. Go get yourself some rest. You sound like you need it."

I lean back against the cushion. "Talk to you later."

He laughs. "Bye Nor."

Chapter 14

The door hinges' squeak is just loud enough to make it back to my bedroom where I'm frantically pinning part of my hair back. I should have made myself get out of bed in time for church this morning, and this would have already been done.

"Nor?" I jump at James's voice and jab the bobby pin into the side of my head.

I rip a second bobby pin from between my teeth and slide it over the one already in my hair. "Be right there!" My palms feel sticky now.

He doesn't say anything more, but I'm pretty sure I hear a chair scoot across the floor. It's just Mexican food, surely this shirt is nice enough.

Did he wonder what to wear too? I bat the idea away and run a hand over the bottom of my socked-foot before sliding it into my boots. Before rounding the corner into the kitchen I adjust my pant legs on my boots.

It's just James.

James stands to his feet fast enough that he has to steady the chair. "You look nice."

I duck my head as my cheeks flare red. "Don't act like you've never seen my hair down." So much for it being *just James* I guess.

He chuckles. Then he gives me one of those awkward side hugs that no one knows how to do. "Well, should we go?"

I swallow. "Yeah." The word comes out wobbly. I push the straw hat that I never wear down on my head. Maybe I shouldn't wear it tonight. It's already on my head though, so I step out the door.

James pulls the door closed behind us and leads the way to his shiny red pickup. It probably sees the road about as much as my personal one has these last several months. He opens the passenger door for me, and I mumble a quiet "thank you" once I'm inside.

My lungs aren't retaining much oxygen as I watch him walk around the front of the pickup. I wipe my palms on my jeans, but they stay clammy.

Why is this such a big deal? It's just James. And we're just going to eat some Mexican food so he can feel like a good friend that's trying to keep me from burying myself.

I swallow. I kinda actually do need a friend to do that.

He starts the engine, and with it comes the soft whine of a fiddle through the speakers. I put my hat in my lap and lean back against the seat so he doesn't have to try to see through me while backing out.

Eyes fixed on the mirror, James's voice is just loud enough to hear over the rumble. "Did you get your leak found the other week?"

Leak? What leak? I try to recall when that falls in the order of fires I've been putting out. After a long squirmy pause my brain gets on track. "Yeah, it was right between the trough and the reservoir. Just a little poly splice and it was good to go."

He looks both ways and pulls out on the highway. "Do you have one of those fancy tools that does the work for you?"

"I wouldn't put it that way, but yes. I have a little poly welder."

A smirk parts his lips, and he rests his wrist over the top of the steering wheel. He looks so relaxed, but I feel like my nerves are crawling inside me.

Grasping for something to fill in the silence, I recall the dog he said he got. "How are you and your pup getting along?"

"Oh, Ranger and I are getting it worked out. After he chewed up half the door on my bathroom cabinet, I built him a pen outside to stay in when I can't take him with me."

I roll my eyes with a laugh. "How much other stuff has he torn up?"

"Hey now." He holds his hand up almost like a stop sign. "Don't be hating on Ranger."

I throw up my hands in surrender but go ahead and laugh. "Alright, alright. Y'all are getting it worked out. I hear you." I snicker one more time before looking out the window to get my amusement under control just as we pull into the parking lot.

James leads the way into the busy little building. It's crowded, but not the worst that I've seen it. At least I'm not running into people when I turn around. James points at a booth in the corner. I nod and follow him through the maze of tables.

I slide in the opposite side from him and put my hat in the booth beside me. *Words, now would be a good time to show up.* But they don't and several awkward moments pass by.

Finally my brain starts working again. "We never did talk about your first sorting. How'd that turn out for you?"

James's face crinkles with a chuckle. "It was interesting."

The waitress picks this exact moment to walk up. All bubbly, she lays menus in front of us and asks what we're drinking. We've both been here enough we don't have to search for options across the plastic-coated pages. Unsweet tea for the both of us.

As she walks away, I fold my hands in my lap and look across the table at James. He looks up from the menu and shakes his head with a grin.

Instead of words coming out of his mouth, he just goes back to reading the menu. *Really? What about the rest of the story?* I don't need the menu, but I scan it. Three times. Still, James says nothing.

I lay it on the table and stare across at him. "So are you going to tell me the story, or do I have to go pry it out of Mindi or George?"

James's eyes appear over the top of the menu. "Oh, the sorting?"

A table full of people leaving behind James distracts me for a second. "Yes, the sorting." *You pain.*

"Well, Nute decided town wasn't his thing right off the bat, and we went crow hopping through the middle of everyone warming up."

My laugh comes out in a burst that lights my cheeks on fire, and my hand covers my mouth. The picture is just so clear in my mind. The light little palomino trying to be broncy. He doesn't even know how to kick up when he feels good.

"I ended up with some kid that hasn't seen a cow outside of those exact pens, as my partner. Between that and Nute being an idiot the whole time, it was pretty awful."

I try to keep from smirking, but it just won't stuff out of the way. "I'm sorry." I slip my hand over my curved lips. "Did you at least laugh?"

The waitress interrupts our banter, setting two glasses of iced tea on the table, straws beside them. "What can I get y'all to eat?"

"Can I have your beef quesadillas?" The gal scribbles on her notepad and nods then she looks to James. "And for you?"

"I'll have the same, please."

She does her same scribble and nod routine. "Absolutely! We'll have those right out." The squeak of her tennis shoes on the old tile fades away.

James tears the paper away from his straw and slides it in his tea. "Yeah, I did get a good laugh in."

"Good, that's all that counts." My fingers start to intertwine with each other. Maybe next month I can make it to the sorting, but I hardly know what day it is anymore. There's very little promise things are going to slow down anytime soon.

We're back to a pause in the conversation. My eyes bounce from one painting on the wall to a table across the room and then a different one.

At least this meal shouldn't be as awkward as some of the ones I've had here.

Halfway through my plate of quesadillas, my phone starts buzzing on the leather seat. Lip between my teeth, I glance down at it. Just before I click it off I read the name across the top. Denise. My heart comes to a sliding stop, heaves, and takes off again. I glance across the table at James.

"Take it if you need to, Nor," he says gently.

"It's Denise." The words come out soft and shaky.

"Take it."

I slide the green circle and lift the phone to my ear. My index finger covers the other ear. "Hello."

"Hey Nora, I'm sorry to call. I hope I didn't interrupt anything." Her voice is hesitant.

Glancing around at the dozen tables in the room I wonder how much she hears. "You're good. What's up?"

"Ian thinks Gentry is trying to colic and we're out of Banamine."

Gentry, Gentry, Gentry. Obviously a horse, but why am I drawing such a blank.

I'm grasping for straws to remember who Gentry is, but regardless, I have medicine. "I think I have some at the house I can bring some over and give him a shot."

Oh, yes, Kayla's palomino.

"Could you? I hate to ask, but..." She doesn't finish.

I nod even though she can't see. My heart doesn't know whether to run off or stay still. I can't very well say no, but now I have to tell James. "Of course. Give me twenty or thirty minutes and I'll be out there with it."

"Thank you!"

I hang up and lay my phone on the two inches of open table top. I'm supposed to be hanging out with James. After a long drink of tea, I glance at him. His eyes stare deeply in mine for the half a second I let them connect.

"Do you mind taking me home?"

By the time the words are out of my mouth, his hat is on his head and he's fishing keys out of his pocket. "Sure, what's up?"

"One of Ian's horses—" His daughter's horse actually, but that's too long of a story to relay right now—"Is trying to colic and he's out of Banamine."

A waitress that's not even ours is walking past, and James waves her down. "Can we get a couple to-go boxes and our check please?"

"Absolutely, give me just a second." She flashes a tired smile and is off.

James jumps right back in. "I have some at the house. We can swing by there on the way to Ian's. It'll be closer."

A smile pushes my cheeks up. A soft one that I give with hugs when people say thoughtful things that 'thank you' isn't a good enough answer for. This time I don't give the accompanying hug though. "Are you sure you don't mind?"

"Not at all." He jingles the keys and looks over his shoulder toward the kitchen.

In a matter of minutes we're out the door and on the road. James drives with an urgency I've only seen from him a handful of times in all the years we worked together.

James's pickup rolls to a stop beside the barn below his house. His pickup door is open the second the wheels stop moving, and I'm high stepping it right behind him. My eyes flick around the cobweb decorated room following the buzzing bee he's turned into. The fridge pops open, a draw screeches, and then James is still for a moment as he draws the medicine up.

Not more than a minute and a half later, James holds up a syringe with clear liquid in it. "Ready?"

"Yeah," I murmur and hot foot it back to the cab. *That was fast.*

I sit on the edge of my seat until my back screams at me and I have to relax back against the cushion. Fifteen minutes later, we turn off the black top. I sit up again.

I swallow the stickiness in my mouth. I never know what to do seeing Ian these days.

The wheels stop turning, and I push the passenger door open. James comes around the front of his pickup, syringe in hand.

I reach the gate in two long strides, James close on my heels. The latch squeals as I pull it back. The little white rocks become fewer and then fade into soft powdered earth inside the fence.

Ian stands a few yards away, a ghostly frame with hollow eyes. He leads the stocky palomino on the back side of the long pen. Making a U-turn, he starts our direction.

"Damn."

My head snaps to my left. James's cheeks are pale even after the trek, and his throat bobs. My mouth turns sticky and I reach up to put my hand on his arm. I change my mind but not before my fingertips have grazed his sleeve just a little.

"Sorry," I mumble. I don't know what I'm apologizing for—not accurately preparing James? Or for brushing his arm?

Ears burning, my eyes glaze over as Ian and James shake hands in front of me. Ian's firm hug around my shoulders brings me back to life.

"Hey," leaves my lips almost inaudibly. Looking past the brim of my hat and up at him, I feel my legs weaken. The dullness in his eyes is a punch to my gut every time. "Gentry is feeling a little finicky, is he?"

"Probably got into a weed."

James takes the guard off the needle and thumps it a couple times. Ian holds out the lead rope in my direction. My eyebrows scrunch together, but I take it anyway.

One hand under Gentry's chin, the other rubbing his forehead, I feel the palomino tense the moment James taps the syringe.

"Easy, buddy," I murmur under my breath.

James runs a finger down the gelding's neck. He finds a spot, taps twice, and slips the needle in. Gentry jerks his head up and takes a couple steps back.

"Easy," James's voice soothes. He draws out a bit of blood and then slowly pushes the Banamine in the vein. "All done."

I lead Gentry in a small circle and then into a full lap around the outside of the pen. On the back end, I slip his halter off. As soon as I step away, he walks to the corner and drops his head. I eye him for a moment, but he doesn't lay down to roll. *Poor boy.*

Still watching him to make sure he doesn't drop and roll, I tie the halter back. A stream of water hits the back of my thigh. I spin around and squint at James. His back to me, I'm pretty sure his shoulders are shaking.

You do that buddy.

Moving on the toes of my boots, I sneak up behind him, fill my cupped hands with water from the trough and throw it towards his shoulder. He turns just as I throw it, and it hits his arm. A girlish giggle leaves my lips.

"What was that for?"

I laugh and skirt around him wide, but not wide enough that the stream of water from the syringe can't reach me. This time it hits my belly. "That! That's what it was for."

A mischievous grin lights up his face. I take it as my cue to leave and duck around the corner of the saddle house. Thank goodness I check where I'm going when I do, because I narrowly miss plowing straight over Ian and Denise sitting on five gallon buckets.

Ian's grin tells me he knows exactly what's happening and is enjoying every minute of it.

I lean against the wall panting for breath.

James comes around the corner a moment later. The syringe appears to be empty, but I still duck when he lifts it to his side.

He laughs. "Jumpy are we?"

Biting back a smile, I step inside the saddle house to hang up the halter. I poke my head out. "Just a little."

"I didn't mean to interrupt you kids' evening."

James squats just down the wall from Ian. "Ah, don't worry about it. I'm glad we got him a shot this early. Maybe it'll give him enough relief that he won't twist a gut."

"I sure appreciate it." Ian scratches figures in the dirt with an old piece of wire. No one says anything for a long minute.

I watch the palomino turn his head toward his belly. He's not quite over it yet.

Finally Ian speaks up again, "We should be good on feed for a while. Sam brought a couple pallets after he closed the feed store yesterday."

I melt next to Ian's perch. I don't even try to squat on the balls of my feet but just plop down in the dirt. "Really? That's nice of him." And just something that Sam would do.

IN BETWEEN PASTURES 129

Ian nods, but there's not the light I expected to see in his eyes. Is he feeling bad? I mean he has to be, but worse than he normally does? Or is it about the feed? He doesn't like asking for help anymore than I do.

The weight is back sitting on the middle of my chest and maybe a little guilt has joined it.

How did I let myself get so carefree when Ian doesn't even know what his tomorrow looks like?

Chapter 15

I smell the last of the fancy thick-cut deli meat that Mom left and wrinkle my nose. *A little sour.* I chunk it in the trash and fish a bowl of chicken salad out of the fridge. Dad's words ring back through my head.

Ian's lucky to have you.

Is he though? Is anyone? At this very moment, some of Clay's cows are inches from being out of water, Tripod and his momma are out of hay, I don't know the last time I reset his splint, and I'm about two days away from being without clean underwear.

Is anyone lucky to have me around?

Not even bothering to grab a plate, I wrap my dirt-caked fingers around the sandwich and walk out the door. Maybe I can make it to the hardware store before they close for lunch.

On my way out the drive, I hit the hole that's been growing in the middle of the road just wrong enough to send my half-finished coffee sloshing out of the cup. I wipe the console off with what's left of my worn out button down's sleeve. Almost laying my sandwich on the still-damp console, I change my mind and hold it between my teeth while I throw the rest of the coffee out the window.

Several miles later, I make a hard right turn into the hardware store parking lot. I don't even bother trying to get close to the door, just whip into a parking spot out in the boonies and hot-foot it for the door.

As the sliding door squeaks open, I fish for my list in my front shirt pocket and realize I'm still holding a piece of sandwich. Man, I must be a sight to watch coming in here. I shove the last of the sandwich in my mouth and straighten out the crinkled paper.

Wiping my palms on my three-day old jeans, I beeline for the plumbing section. I walk a couple aisles before I find where the PVC parts end and the poly fittings begin. The barbed nipples I need are on the bottom rack, all lined up every size you could possibly want. My knees grind a little as I squat down. The sideways shuffle it takes to get over to the one inch ones just about does my knees in.

I grab four of the metal fittings. Juggling them all in one little hand of mine, I stand and scan the shelf for the other part I need. Out of the corner of my eye, I see a person on the other end of the aisle. I stack a couple more fittings in my hand and turn—right smack-dab into James Butler.

Metal fittings bounce off the cement floor, making a high-pitched cling each time. I wince as I scramble to pick them up. James squats down in front of me and catches one before it has the chance to clang a second time.

"Sorry, I wasn't paying attention." The words come half muffled out of my mouth.

His fingers graze mine as we grab at the same fitting. "It's alright. I've been going to come by and see you anyway. This works just as well." He nods to my handful. "What's all this for anyway?"

I take the ones he's collected and cradle them in my arm. "Water line screwed up where it switches from metal to poly."

"That's no good. Need some help?"

I shake my head. "I can get it." I turn to leave the aisle like I originally was, only this time I go the opposite direction.

"Nora."

I stop. James comes around in front of me. I force myself to look up and meet his piercing gaze. He can probably see clean through to the parts behind me as intense as those blue eyes are.

"What's going on?"

My eyebrows pinch together.

"I've called you a half dozen times in the last week, left you voicemails, even stopped by your house. I can't track you down to save my life." His fingers curl and uncurl around the metal store shelf. "I'm just trying to make sure you're okay."

My shoulders slump. I know he's been calling, and I haven't been answering. "I've been busy." I look down at the mud that has turned half of my jean legs gray and then lift my handful of parts. "Prime example, the cows I'm trying to get water back to. I don't have time to talk on the phone."

His big hands almost grasp his straw hat. Stopping short of doing so, they curl into fists.

My heart drops further. If it keeps doing that it's going to wear a hole in the bottom of my boot and just leave all together. "I'm sorry."

His eyes flick from the brim of my hat to my cracked muddy shoes, but he avoids my gaze. "What else do you need?"

I look up at him for a long moment. Why's he still trying to help? I just brushed him off *again*. Fishing my list out again, I hand it to him.

"Next aisle will have most of that. I'll help you carry it to the front."

I'm not sure if he's blind, stupid, or just too persistent for his own good, but I've never seen James take no for an answer. I don't try this time, just follow him around the corner and nod when he lifts things from the shelf.

At the counter James lays all the parts out. "There you are. Catch you later." He waves to the approaching cashier and our eyes meet for a moment. Then his long legs are eating up the grungy tile in a few strides he's out the doors empty handed.

"Uh, okay, thank you," I call.

I watch him disappear into the morning sunlight and then shake my head. I'm not even going to try to figure that man out. He's a mystery, and I'll leave it at that.

Cigarette smoke overwhelms me as the cashier strolls to the faded counter. "Anything else for you today?"

"No sir, that'll be it." For now, anyway. Let's hope I don't have to come back.

The clerk rattles off a number, and I slip the ranch credit card in the machine. She hands me a receipt and a double bagged sack of parts.

Off I go again. But before I leave town, I slip by the gas station and fuel up. Then I head back down Fm 1676 and along the haphazard dirt road to the house.

Rolling up the driveway, I squint. What is on the porch? I don't have porch decorations. *Please don't let it be a dog.* I can not add one more thing depending on me right now.

A few more dusty rolls of the tires and I can make out the shape of a man. I glance over in the seat for the handle of my pistol. It's in place. The shape of the hat brim becomes clear and my muscles stop bristling just a little.

James. *At least it isn't some hobo that wandered up.*

I push the pickup door open and swing my feet to the ground, water jug in hand. "What are you doing out here?"

James drags one boot across the dust covering my ragged front porch. "Just happened by."

Well I guess he's not too mad at me.

A huff of a laugh leaves my chest. "Right, because you have so much to do out this direction." I stub one boot and then the other on the porch, dirt flying with each tap.

Two sure steps and he's in front of me. Reaching out, he leans my hat back on my head a touch. "Nor, you don't get to do all this by yourself anymore. If you're going to run me off and keep me out of your life, it's going to have to be with that pistol you carry around."

Words pop off one another in my mind. "I—" I lick the dust off my lips. "I'm not trying to run you..." I don't finish. I guess I kinda was.

I grab the wooden post next to me and try to reframe my words. Just above his head is an old wasp nest, I should probably knock that down. Focusing, I look at his nose. "Thank you for being a good friend."

I lift the water jug in my hand. "I've got to fill this up and then go to the pump. Want to come inside?"

One big step back and he's turning the doorknob. The hinges squeak as he pushes the wooden door in. "After you."

Back in the pickup, James props his arm up on the back of the bench seat, and I ease off the brake. "So tell me again how this water line is all messed up?"

"It comes out of the pump with a nipple. And then a coupling and an elbow and forty-seven other pieces." The brakes squeal as we ease through a dried out rut in the two-track road. "Then it eventually gets into poly, which runs the rest of the way to the trough and out to the trough on the back side of the pasture."

He nods a couple of times. "Someone sure did get creative, didn't they?"

"I don't know how or which happened first, but the poly split about a hundred yards from the pumphouse and one of the couplings—or maybe the elbow—one of them rusted out." I glance over at his concentrating face that could double as a mean-mug. "It's like a darn lake out there."

"Ah man!"

I flinch at his uproar.

He points to his holey leather shoes. "Why didn't you tell me that? I can't get these shoes wet."

I stare at his straight face for a couple seconds before my lips spread in a grin. I shake my head.

He nudges my elbow with his. "That was a good one, huh?"

Staring straight ahead, I don't dare meet his playful gaze. It would only encourage him.

We pull around to the uphill side of the pump house. A hundred yards out from the other side of the cinderblock building water shines in the sun. "What do you think of our lake?"

Leaning over and rolling up his pant legs, he grunts out, "Pretty good start to one anyway."

Looking down at my own legs and rubber-covered feet I wave a dismissive hand. Old pants and rubber boots. They've already been wet and muddy once today they'll survive another round.

As soon as I step out of the pickup, I sink down into the mud until half my boots are covered. The couple steps I have to take to get into the pump house are like slogging through syrup, but I finally make it to the ply-wood door.

"What's first?"

"I've been wondering that since I saw all this the first time." I chuckle and sling the door open.

I give James the rundown again, this time pointing out to him the pieces I bought replacements for. He nods along.

"That poly looks like it's drained out. You want to get it done first? That inside the pump house is going to be a bigger project."

"Sounds good."

Bent over with a pipe wrench in my hand, I'm surprised I hear my phone ringing in the pickup cab. I lay the wrench over the poly pipe and slog over to the device before it stops ringing. The call is from Ian. My hands are too wet to tap the screen, though. By the time I wipe my hands on the back of my pants and try again, the screen fades into the sunset picture of my lockscreen and the ringing stops.

I groan and wipe my phone on my shirt again before trying to call him back. It rings a couple times before he picks up.

"Hello." Ian's new voice—weak and distant—barely fills up the phone line.

"Hey, sorry I couldn't get my phone to answer." I lean back against the pickup.

"That's alright. Are you busy?"

I roll my lips between my teeth and look around at the mud. Well, kinda. But Ian doesn't ask that just for fun. "Not too bad, what you got?"

"There's some papers at the house in the safe that I need. Could you run them up here?"

I rub my mud-caked palm on my jeans and look back at the tools leaned up against the pump-house wall. "Uh, yeah, when do you need them by?"

He pauses a moment, and I hear low muffled voices in the background. "Just before five if you can."

James appears, wiping his hands on a filthy rag. "Go," he mouths.

I nod my head at him. The tools and standing water stare me down. I don't know how it's going to all get done, but I'll take the papers. "I need to finish up a few things here and then I'll be on my way."

"Alright, call me when you get to the house, and I'll walk you through how to get into the safe."

"Sounds good."

"Thank you, girl."

I nod even though he can't see it. "See you in a bit." After slipping my phone into my pocket, I run a hand down my face. Mud is already splattered over it, nobody will notice a little bit more.

James shuffles his feet in the damp dirt beside the back tire. "I can get this if you need to head out."

"Uh, no," I stammer and pick at the mud on my hands. "I can get this done. I just need to get over to Ian's in two hours or so."

But there's a half a day's work I still need to do over there. I sigh. "I, uh—" My shoulders crumble.

I take a couple deep breaths. I'll just have to do that stuff when I get back from town. After dark. Headlights and flashlights, they've become my friends lately.

James steps closer, his voice gentle. "What is it, Nor?"

"There are some papers Ian needs today before five, and it just dawned on me everything I'm supposed to do over there today." My hand flails at my side. "I—I'll just have to do it when I get back."

His bear-sized hand rests on my shoulder. "Tell me what needs to be done over at Ian's, and I'll get it covered. You take him what you need to."

His blue eyes are so soft, like a teddy bear instead of the giant grizzly his hands could belong to. I look into those eyes for a just a moment longer before hugging him. "Thank you. You're a lifesaver."

He chuckles, returning the gentle hug. "Anytime, Nor."

An hour later, the water line is pieced back together and we're bouncing over the road back to my house.

"The calf in the pens needs his splint reset. It was halfway off when I was over there a couple days ago. I'm pretty sure they're out of hay too. It's east of the pens. You can't miss it." I drum my fingers on the cracked leather steering wheel. "Um, I think those are the big things."

"Got it." He hangs his arm out the window. Out of the corner of my eye I catch sight of the mischievous smirk on his face.

Never a good sign. What kind of mischief is he up to? I drive on a little ways before glancing over. The look is still there. "What are you grinning about?"

He chuckles. "Just wondering if you're going to town with the war paint on your face."

I narrow my eyes, get over the bump in the two track road, and then swing back to stare at him. "You're pretty painted up yourself, so I wouldn't say too much there."

"Yeah, but I'm not going to town."

I shake my head, a grin now on my own face. "I was feeling bad about putting you to work, but not anymore."

"Good!"

Turning the pickup off next to my house, I take a second and relax back against the seat. What a day, and it's not really that close to being done. I wouldn't be done with that leak if I was doing it by myself though.

I lean back against the seat. "Thanks for your help. It sure went a lot better than it would have."

He nods. "Of course."

A thin smile and a moment more in the protection of the quiet cab, and then I force myself back into the sun.

Pushing the door open, I tuck my pistol in my belt. Halfway to the porch, I freeze. "Whenever you get over to Ian's, why don't you take my ranch pickup?"

"Nah, I can—"

"I'm taking *mine* to town, and I drive the ranch one over there all the time. Clay doesn't care."

He drops a couple tools in the tool box on his pickup. "Alright."

I flash a quick smile. "Thank you. Now I'm going to wash my war paint off, as you called it."

When I step out of the shower, I listen for the squeak of the floorboards or scratch of a chair being pulled back, but I don't hear either. I kinda just abandoned James outside and now have no clue if there is a man in my house or not. *Perfect*.

Thankfully I did have the sense to bring clean clothes into the bathroom with me. I throw them on and pick up my hair brush. With it halfway through my hair, I pad into the kitchen in my sock-clad feet. There is no James, but there is a little bag with a napkin chip-clipped to it.

Don't go hungry.

The brush stops mid-rake. I hold the napkin between my fingers a moment, and my heart flutters a couple light beats. James made me a sandwich?

I finish brushing my hair, throw on a pair of boots, and lay the sandwich on top of my backpack full of things I need to go to town. I turn a full circle in the kitchen but don't see anything else I need to take. If I'm missing anything, I guess I can live without it until I get back.

The screen door bangs closed behind me. I walk past the Chevy to my just as old pickup. Sandwich in mind, I set my backpack in the seat and make sure it's upright instead of tossing it haphazardly. I fish the key from my pocket.

And now to find James.

I crank the engine, and surprisingly it starts on the first try. Since Clay left the old Chevy out here, I haven't used my own more than twice. I pull around by the barn and leave the engine running. Just as I reach the barn door, it opens..

"Goodness gracious." James closes his eyes a prolonged second before stepping off the cement onto the dirt in front of me.

A laugh sputters out of me at his eyes so saucer round.

"Since when do you have such a fancy Spade bit?" The latch on the door slides into place.

"Oh that's new. Found it on Ranch World Ads."

"Dang." He drags the word out. "You've come up in the world."

Strolling the few feet to my pickup, I shrug. "I've been working on my collection." I suddenly don't want to go. Instead I linger, rolling a rock with my town boots.

"Well, you off?" His hands slide snuggly in his front pockets.

I glance up and nod. "I guess so. Are you sure you don't mind doing all this? I can—"

"I don't mind." He swings my pickup door open. "You go to town and tend to that."

"Alright." I take one long step forward, but then pull myself short. Instead, I extend an arm that's a little more limber than a stick out in an awkward hug. "Thanks."

"Anytime." He reaches around me with a grin. "Now get."

A little laugh bubbles out of me, and I jump into the cab. He closes the door and waves.

He'll figure out how to start the skid steer with the screwdriver, right? I pick up my phone. *No, he's a grown man and more than capable.*

Chapter 16

The air is thick enough with disinfectant that my lungs should be clean in two breaths. *Looks like I'm at the right place.* I step forward to the long desk and one of the curly-headed ladies behind it.

"Hi, what can I do for you?"

I produce the stack of papers from below the counter. My shirt sleeve catches on a pen in a cup and three others topple out. I wince. "I need to drop these off. They're Ian Kelly's documents."

Her bright red nail polish is blinding against the white of the paper. I scramble to stuff the pens back where they belong while she scans the first few pages. "I'll get them on his records. Thank you."

"Thank you." The chairs of the waiting room blur by until the heavy wooden office door slows me down. The air outside isn't fresh like at home where I can pick out three different bushes and manure, but it's better than that cloud of chemicals.

After a quick look at the directions Ian texted me, I pull out of the office parking lot and turn left. *White house, green trim, with enough space to park a car on either side of it.* Man, I like his directions.

A couple more turns back into the neighborhood and I spot Denise's little red SUV. As I pull up behind it I see the space Ian was talking about— three lawn mower widths of grass between their rental and the houses on either side of it. I grin a little. I bet Ian noticed that before the car was even in park.

Each step up the walk is like its own commitment. I haven't seen Ian in nearly a week. What has the treatment done to his body? Almost everyone I know says it gets worse before it gets better.

I swallow. How much worse? How much worse is there *to* get?

Ready or not we're committed now. I knock twice on the door and then turn the knob. The bird hanging on it thunks against the wood as Denise's "come in" drifts out. I put on a smile before stepping over the threshold.

"Hey, Nora." Denise wraps me in a hug, long and tight. I return it, a lump forming in my throat, until she loosens her grip.

Turning into the depths of the house, she leads me past a blue bird drawing in the entryway. "Thank you for bringing those papers. Did they give you any trouble at the office?"

"Not at all." The cream walls turn to pale blue ones as we round the corner into a kitchen and dining area. Bird pictures and paintings of various sizes are sprinkled on the walls. "How are you doing?"

"It's been a long week already, but we're hanging in there."

Dad's words come back to me. *He's hanging in there. Has a good attitude about it all.* Would it be any harder if everyone just said what they actually mean? I guess I don't want to say the real words either though. James didn't get them when he asked me.

Not this time. But he has.

A neat stack of dishes are in the drain and an empty paper towel roll behind it. I should have asked her if she needed things from the house. Surely there are things she's missing. Next time.

Light streams in the windows bringing to life the nature theme. My eyes stop roaming to study a bird painting with a quote on the bottom.

'No bird soars too high if he soars with his own wings.'

It might be better if it said something about when the bird's own wings aren't enough, but they didn't ask me when they chose the quote.

"Hey girl." Ian's voice is a rasp. Not the big bold declaration that's met me through phone lines and across driveways.

I freeze a moment. If his body is as weak as his voice, this week has been harder on him than I thought. I round the corner of the couch. "Hey." I point to a round butterscotch-candy pillow propping up his feet on the couch. "You have comfort and style around here."

He tosses one of the plush candy pieces at me. "You like that?"

I turn the pillow over in my hands, throat so tight I have to swallow several times before I can speak. "Pretty fancy."

"Sit. You're making me nervous."

Me making him nervous? I feel like a long-tailed cat in a room full of rocking chairs. There's two seating options. A white canvas chair with a tall back and those studded button things in the back of it, and a blue velvety one. It's a good thing I showered before I came, since normally I'm every range of filthy. Still, I barely even perch on the light chair.

"Well, what have you been up to?" Ian reaches for a mason jar glass, taking a long drink of a green smoothie.

Where to start. "Between the idiots that keep driving through fences and old pipelines I can't get anything fun done."

"Oh boy." The glass wobbles in the air as Ian replaces it on the end table.

My eyebrows arch. "Speaking of fun, I can't get Clay's cows to stay in the back of that corner pasture. There's some grass for them to clean up, but they won't stay there more than a day or two."

He shifts on the couch. "Ah, they might be needing some mineral and salt back there. Or they think water is too far, but that's not something you can do a whole lot about."

I study his thinned, yellow face that lights up the moment he starts talking about cattle. Melting back into the chair, I forget all about doctors and hospitals and the to-do list waiting for me. Right now it's just me and Ian.

"I need to get some mineral out for them. I'll move it back there to that corner and see what they do."

Ian tugs the pillow out from under his now-scrawny legs and swings them to the floor. He sits upright a minute before speaking. "How's that calf doing?"

I shuffle my weight in the chair and study the stitches on my shoes. "Well I left James to tend to him today, but he's been making good progress. I think his momma might even be putting on some weight."

"Good. It wouldn't hurt to put a little more meat on their bones." He picks up the mason jar and takes a couple slow swallows. This time he makes a face as it goes down. "Darn greens are supposed to work wonders." He lifts the glass and points it at me before putting it down.

A grin quirks one side of my lips up. Handiest cowman this side of the Pecos river, but has to defend his drink.

"How is James?"

My hands intertwine. There's enough mud under my fingernails to pot a plant. "He's good. I guess Wade doesn't have much going on to keep him busy. He helped me with a water leak nearly all morning."

Ian's eyebrows shoot up, and I look away. Not before I feel heat shoot up my neck and onto my cheeks though. And for what? We fixed a water leak. Real glamorous.

"That's good. I'm glad you're letting him help you. He seems like a real nice kid."

James is no kid, but I guess Ian is old enough to be both of our dads.

Denise calls that supper is ready. I stand and wait for Ian to put the pillows back in order on the couch before slowly rising to his feet. I try not to let myself think about how much of that is to cover something else up.

Just make it through supper and then you can cry all the way home.

***

Halfway home, the oncoming headlights thin out, and I relax back against the seat. The wind coming in my barely cracked window picks up James's sandwich bag and drifts it to the floor board. I glance at it every chance the road will let me. *Why did he make me a sandwich?*

Ian's got one thing right for sure: James is a good guy. Always has been.

"I'm just trying to make sure you're okay." The tenderness in that comment from James still makes heat climb my throat even now.

Even Ian made a comment after I mentioned James. *"I'm glad you're letting him help."*

I pull my bottom lip between my teeth. Would Ian still be glad James is helping me if he knew that I sent James a book of a text about my fears? Meanwhile, sometimes I'm too tired to even have a conversation with Ian.

The radio plays a sad slow Waylon Jennings song. I cock my head.

Poor James. "Goodness gracious, I've been awful."

One minute I practically pour my entire jumbled up jar of feelings to him and the next I won't answer his phone calls. "God, you've made one heck of a persistent human being out of him."

Chapter 17

Fumbling with coffee grounds through half open eyes, I spill half a scoop on the counter. *Amazing*. Grounds in my palm, I lift it to my nose. I breathe in only to get the faintest hint of the fresh coffee smell. *Darn head congestion*.

Waiting on the coffee, I pull my favorite sweatshirt over my oversized t-shirt and perch on the counter beside the coffee pot. Leaning against the cabinets, my mind runs through the day's looming to do list. First up is moving Ian's cows. It should have been done several days ago.

The coffee pot beeps, telling me it's done. I fill a mug, wrap both hands around it, and breathe in the steam. Sinking into my brown chair, I keep my aching eyes closed while sipping the scalding liquid.

I move my Bible from the table beside me to my lap. Blindly pulling back pages and feeling around until I find my bookmark, I manage to open it to Job.

Another sip of coffee helps me read the first few sentences. The more I read, the stronger my headache pounds. Two more sentences, and I lay my head back.

God, I can't read right now.

Another couple sips of coffee.

In fact I don't know that I am even going to keep a train on the thought rails enough to pray.

My coffee has cooled off enough that I can now consume it in gulps without burning all my taste buds off. It may not be helping my headache, but at least it is soothing my throat a little bit. I down that cup and then pry myself out of the cushions.

Mug refilled, I take myself to the bedroom. I find the most worn out pair of jeans in my closet and pull them on. A hand-me-down pearl snap from my dad isn't as comfortable as the blue 'Courage Cowgirl' t-shirt I slept in, but it'll do.

I top off my coffee so it's nice and steaming and then head out the door. I make it about five steps off the porch and turn around. I do not need this sweatshirt out here. I shirk it inside the door and then head back out.

Inside the barn door, I pry my fingers out of their coffee cup mold to pour the geldings' feed. The pellets banging against the bottom of the bucket makes my brain pound against my head harder than it already was.

The boys are waiting on me at the gate, clustering around as I fiddle with the latch. Banks nickers a little. The latch catches, and when I jerk it loose, my pinky smashes right between the latch and the pipe of the gate. A string of words that don't even make sense together run through my brain while I suck air between my teeth to keep the jumble from coming out.

Finally I shake my hand and drag in some of the air I just blew out. *Good Lord have mercy that was enough to make a grown man cry.*

Through the gate, I push it closed. I'll deal with the latch in a minute. The horses press closer to me the nearer the trough I get. I manage to pour the feed out without my shoe getting stepped on and drag myself back to the barn. I gulp coffee, trying to get to the hot part for it to soothe my already screaming throat.

Dad always swore most sickness could be cured with a trip outside. Closing the door, I start to shake my head, feeling the pressure jostle around like a soup can. I think this one is going to take more than one trip outside, and maybe more than one day.

Regardless, I fix myself some oatmeal, doctor it up with honey and peanut butter, and start picking at it. I beg each bite to infuse strength into my limbs that refuse to feel alive. Instead, it gets harder to swallow.

I read the big white numbers across my phone screen. 9:38 am. I'm never this late to feed and get my day started. My spoon screeches across the bottom of the bowl. *Gah lee, that's awful.* I drop the spoon from my hand and pick up my phone.

Pulling up my recent calls, I don't even have to scroll to find James's name. It lights up bright red with the date from two days ago—right before he showed up on my porch to help me fix the water leak. He wasn't kidding when he said he'd been trying to check on me.

My finger hovers over his name. Ian's cows can't go another day without being moved. I lay the device down and snatch up the snot rag on the corner of the table. The material absorbs the little trickle of snot, but when I blow, I don't even have to look to know that's a glob of green goup.

I swallow another gulp of semi-hot coffee. I should really change over to hot tea now that I've consumed a whole pot of caffeine. Picking up my phone again, I hit the five letter name.

The little trill ring makes my heart beat faster every time it starts over. About the fifth time there's a scuffle and then a "hello".

"Hey," I clear my throat.

"Oh hey, Nor, what's up?"

I scoot the snot rag over my nose, but it turns out just to be a phantom run. "You wouldn't happen to be able to move Ian's cows for me, would you?"

"Today?" His voice comes through the line clearer than his 'hello'.

I swallow. *Just do it, Nora.* "Yes."

More scuffling comes through the phone line. "Uh, yeah, I probably can." Muttering follows. I've done enough of it myself to know it isn't for me. "How far do they need to go?"

"Just in the next pasture over." I clear my throat again. "If you're too busy it's okay."

Metal clatters in the distance. "Dadgummit, stand up!"

I cringe. I think I picked the worst possible time to call him. Before I find words to tell him never mind he's talking again.

"It'll be late this afternoon before I can get over there but I can sure do it for you." This time his voice has evened out.

"That'll work. I would—" My throat takes things in its own hands and makes me cough up the lung I've been trying to keep in me.

The second I quit coughing long enough for him to, James asks, "Nor, are you okay?"

"I think I got ran over by a truck." I rasp out, reaching for my mug.

He chuckles a little but cuts it short. "I think if you got ran over you wouldn't be talking to me. What can I bring you?"

The edges of my lips perk up just a little bit. "Nothing, I just need to close my eyes."

"Be sure to drink plenty. I'll check on you here after a while."

Always checking on me. "Okay."

"Alright, I'll talk to you later."

"Thank you," I get out after another cough.

"Anytime, Nor."

As soon as those three beeps let me know the phone line is dead, I empty my head of every drop of snot that will blow out and then melt into my brown chair. I pull a blanket over the top of me and my knees up to my ears. In moments I'm out of it.

***

Hazy-eyed, I look around the room. My house—living room—broad daylight. The sudden urge to cough brings it all together so clearly. I make a pit stop and then drag myself to the kitchen.

The coffee pot is empty. *What a shame.* I dump the ground out and run straight water through it. While it gurgles the last drops, I lift my phone. 2:45 reads across the top of the screen. And I still feel like I could sleep another five hours.

There's a stack of messages on the screen too. James and Mindi's names appear more than once. I type out a quick 'I didn't die' message and answer James's question about Ian's cattle. Mindi's messages stare me down.

Another horse club thing I'll miss. This time it's a meeting, but I don't know if that's worse or better than missing an event. I was hoping to keep up with meetings and watch the kids at a couple playdays. Neither has happened since Mindi got the guys to cover practices.

I scoot a mug over to get a wooden spoon. A whole avalanche of plates, bowls, and utensils clatter down. Bending down to scoop them up, I have to reach for the counter top to steady myself while the pressure in my head sloshes around like an overturned water trough. I sink onto the floor and close my eyes.

Of all the days. It all comes crashing down—literally—today.

It takes several minutes before I can stand. Dishes still on the ground, I finish making my tea. Taking it and my phone to the living room, I nestle back into my brown chair. I pull up Mindi's message and stare at the blinking space for my return one.

I am sorry I won't be able to make it tonight. I think I have the flu.

Send. A fresh message box and cursor blinking cursor stare at me. I gulp another burning mouthful of tea.

I can't keep up with everything right now and I don't want the horse club to take the hit of that. I need to step back from the club right now.

I reread it. It sounds professional, right? Halfway through combing the lines again my phone starts ringing. It's Denise. I gulp tea to soothe my throat and tap the green circle. "Hello."

"Hey, how's it going?"

I swallow the tickle in my throat. "Been better." The tickle does not leave and makes me cough a couple times. "I think I picked up the flu somewhere."

"Oh no, I'm sorry. Do you have tea?"

I raise the mug in my hand in a silent sign. "Drinking it now."

"Good."

Momentarily setting the mug on the apple crates that double as a little coffee table, I tug the blue and brown horse blanket from behind me. "What's up?"

A defeated sigh rides the phone line. "Ian's been worrying about money."

I freeze with the mug halfway to my lips. *Of course he is, these treatments can't be cheap.*

"He's thinking about selling Sailor to pay for part of this treatment."

Selling Sailor. I shake my head and then regret it when the tidal waves start rolling. Ian hadn't said anything about it when I talked to him for an hour and a half just two nights ago.

Wind crackles through the line and then becomes distant. "I've told him we can sell some of my dad's old guns, but he won't hear of it."

I snuggle deeper into my chair. "Sailor will bring a pretty penny. He probably wants to take one hit and knock out what he needs instead of pedaling a bunch of little things."

Sometimes the man is too logical for his own good.

Of all the horses, Sailor makes the most and the least amount of sense to sell. He's the main one Ian rides—his go-to mount. He's in his prime and darn nice to ride. But who will Ian ride when he gets back to it?

"Right." Denise's voice goes in one ear and out the other without interrupting my thoughts at all.

When. Yes, when. There's no *if* he gets back to it.

I swallow hard. Tears well in my eyes. I haven't had enough time with him. He changed my whole world. There will never be enough time with him.

Cool air blows through the vents straight on me. *Darn AC. I could do without it quite so much today.*

I flop the blanket up over my arms. "Do you know what he wants for him?"

She rattles off three different numbers. "I don't know if he's settled on one."

Dang it. It doesn't matter which one of them he settles on, I can't swing it. Even if I sold the old saddle I keep for back up, I can't afford it.

"I don't know if you know anyone..." Her voice trails off.

"I'll see who I can come up with." I drum my fingers on the yellow mug. "James might know of someone." *Maybe he won't. Maybe there's another way around this.*

A gust of wind whips through the speakers again. "I'm going to give your dad and Owen a call too. Between all of us surely we know someone."

Whether from the reality of Sailor leaving or a flair of the flu, dizziness makes me lean back against the cushions.

"I'm sorry, I'm talking on while you're not feeling good. You rest up now."

On que, I cough. "I will."

Off the phone, I down the last of the almost cold tea. The mug clinks against the table top. I hug the blanket close as my eyes burn with tears.

Does it ever stop? Does the giving things up ever come to an end?

Chapter 18

"How are those cattle back in the Valley?" Ian's voice is raspy with weakness, but he perches on the edge of his chair ready for action.

Denise points a stare at him from her rocking chair in the opposite corner of the den. "Honey, she didn't come over here to work."

Ian rolls his eyes a little. "Am I working you too hard?"

A big grin bunches up my cheeks under my eyes. "It's not work. I enjoy it."

He turns back to Denise, and if I'm not mistaken, winks. "The cattle in the valley?"

"They've been staying out in the draw a lot. They only let me coax them in for a bite of feed every other time." My knee aches where it's propped up on my other one. I guess my muscles haven't bounced back a hundred percent since the flu nearly a week ago. "The cows don't look great, but the calves aren't bad at all. I actually think they're about right to ship."

He runs a hand over his mustache.

I flip my phone face up on the leather arm chair to read the time. *11am*. "I've caught some of them up at the water about this time of day before."

"Some fresh air would be good for you." Denise's voice carries a tune, like she could break into song at any moment. She takes her cup from the side table and steps off toward the kitchen.

Ian pushes himself up with a hand on either arm of his chair. In a few steady, if slower than usual, steps and he's gazing out the window by his desk. "It is a pretty day."

"Let's go, then." Denise's voice carries from the kitchen followed by the steady splash of the faucet.

A grin blooms under Ian's mustache. A mustache I sure am glad is still around. Cancer has taken the color from his face and the muscle from his bones, but it hasn't taken that big bushy mustache.

Thank you, Lord.

Ian pulls on his puttering around boots. I abandon the den and lean against the cool kitchen counter next to Denise.

A giddy buzz ripples through my veins when Ian reaches for his hat by the back door. It's been too dang long since I've looked over country with him. Long enough I can't quite recall when it was.

Denise is loaded down with her big cup and two bottles of electrolytes as we head out the door. Ian heads for his fancy Ford and Denise looks over at me.

"We're getting special treatment, taking the big rig," she whispers.

Perched on the edge of the middle seat in the back, I feel like I'm seeing these pastures for the first time. Ian notes changes I've been too busy to notice. The mesquites are losing some of the green from their leaves. The jackrabbits have had a really good year.

My heart beats a little slower, and each breath feels like it has the right amount of oxygen. The wind blowing in the open windows smells a little sweeter.

"Dadgum, nearly forgot where I was going." The pickup makes a sharp left turn nearly throwing me against the door.

I grab the door handle and get straight in the seat again.

Ian whips the long bed around to block the gate out of the water lot. Putting the pickup in park, he hangs one arm out the window. "These calves don't look too bad. Better than what I expected."

They've put on some weight since the last time I saw many of them at one time.

He steps out of the pickup and folds his arms over his chest. I get out of the cab and stand next to him. I scan the scattering of Hereford pairs for what exactly we're studying so hard.

"That cow with the crooked horns has been licking herself."

I bite back a grin. Only Ian would scrutinize a cow from halfway across the lot over her licking herself. I do a little more squinting myself though and see the slicked up places on the red hide. Daddy always said that meant they felt good. I guess it means they feel better than they look sometimes.

"What do you think of those calves?"

I jump a little. I'm still on the cow licking herself. I stuff my hands in my pockets to buy myself a little time.

Ian turns to me now. My heart rate picks up. I already told him I think they might be about shipping size. Did I miss something?

He takes a couple calculated steps around big rocks. "Think they run close to six hundred pounds?"

My eyes are not scales. They would be the worst set of scales you'll ever come in contact with. "Maybe."

"They'll be pretty close." He runs a hand over his mustache again.

I study the calves, sizing them up in reference to the heifers I calved at Wade's and how much they weighed when they'd come freshly weaned. They could be close to six.

With a glance at Ian, I wonder if there's about to be smoke coming out of his ears from how hard his brain is working. He's still steadily staring at the Hereford pairs that have started to lie down under the few mesquites.

"What are you thinking?" *Turn his own question on him.*

A couple seconds tick by, then he slowly swivels his head to look at me. "This little wad of calves will almost be a trailer load."

A whirlwind whips through the water lot, throwing around dust and making me shove my hat farther on my head. "What sale are you thinking of taking them to?"

Ian turns his back against the wind. "Big Spring usually is the best this time of year."

"I could run them over there Tuesday morning if you wanted." I stub up a tiny weed with the toe of my shoe.

"Are you sure?" His voice sounds like he wants to crawl under a rock. In turn I'd like to crawl under a rock for him.

"I'm sure." I amble a few steps forward to lean on a post. "They ought to sell good."

He pulls the pen from his shirt pocket. A few scratches on the palm of his hand and then he nods again. "Alright, if we put out a bale of hay that'll hold them here until then." Rocks grind under his boots as he turns back to the pickup.

I trail behind him like a loyal border collie and hop in the back seat again.

IN BETWEEN PASTURES

The pickup doors closing give my thoughts the permission they didn't need to run full blast. A trailer load of calves will bring a decent check. Depending on exactly what he needs for this round of treatment, it could be pretty dang close to being the funds he needs.

Pretty dang close to Sailor staying here.

The engine revs into the next gear almost drowning out Denise's voice. "What do you think of how they look?"

I'm preoccupied with the little dance party happening in my stomach. I don't pay attention to the rest of their conversation. Ian needs Sailor to be here for when he gets back to riding.

I need Sailor to be here for when Ian gets back to riding.

We bounce out to the backside of the pasture, check the other water, and then circle back to the house. Ian cuts the engine. I step out and leisurely scan the horizon through the heatwaves of late-August, occupying my eyes while Ian gets out of the pickup.

He may be feeling up to a drive through the pasture, but weakness still drags him down. I don't want to watch him struggle through simple tasks anymore than he wants to be watched.

The pickup door clicks closed behind him, then he looks off into the pasture like I have been. "You want to load some hay?"

Something about his casual way of suggesting it gets my feet ready to glide over the rocks. "Sure."

"I'll bring the flatbed around by the barn."

I stretch my strides towards the crumbling hay barn, little white rocks skittering under my leather shoes. Skid steer rattling obnoxiously, I lift the bale up and tilt it down so that it lands on the flat side. It slides off the hay spears and smacks the flatbed a little harder than I was going for. *Yikes.* I push it back just a little closer to the gooseneck ball before buzzing the skid steer back to its place under the shed.

My hands still vibrate when I turn the machine off and step out. Denise is at the edge of the yard, so I stroll over and join her in watching Ian's dust hang in the air.

There's so many things I want to ask her, say to her, but none of the words will come. They're all too heavy to begin sorting through.

Denise drags a folding chair a few feet away from the big oak tree and sits down. "He's so happy to be back out here."

"I bet he gets a little stir crazy in town." I jog over to the side of the house and drag a camping chair next to her.

She scoffs with a shake of her head. "More than a little. He drives me crazy some days. But it makes him rest, which is good."

"Yeah." The word comes out airy. Like a horse stalled up to heal, even if it is the best thing for Ian it's sure hard to watch. He's made for wide open spaces.

"Thanks so much for keeping up with everything out here. Ian talks about the ranch everyday, but he doesn't worry about it." She turns to face me, holding my gaze for a long moment. "That's thanks to you."

I shake my head. I haven't done anything special.

Her hand rests on my arm. "Really. He wouldn't rest that easy with just anyone out here."

My throat bobs with the wad of feelings that are all wrapped up together. *Really, it's my pleasure. Anything to help him get better.*

We move under the big oak tree outside the house and settle into a couple folding chairs. I pick up a stick and twirl it between my fingers.

"Do you think he'll keep Sailor now?" Once the words have left my lips I force my eyes up to look over at Denise.

"Probably. He hasn't said much about it since I mentioned it to you."

"Good," I murmur.

The old pickup rolls to a stop under our tree. Ian strides over to the chairs Denise and I are propped up in, dragging one with him.

"All good?" Denise asks, as he sinks into the mesh.

"They'll be set for the next couple days." His gaze flicks to me. "Are you sure you'll be able to take them Tuesday?"

"Yes sir." There's a lull, so I push to my feet. "I'm going to head out. I've got a set of cows I need to get syrup out to."

"Alright then, leave us." A deep chuckle follows his remark.

Man, I've missed his mischievousness.

Denise holds me in a hug longer than normal for her. I feel my chest tighten at her last squeeze.

"Love you, girl." His gaze pierces mine and his Adam's apple bobs before he pulls me into a hug.

I squeeze him as tight as I dare since I can nearly overlap my arms all the way around him now. "Love you too." I pull back from the hug and meet his gaze for one fleeting second. "Get some rest this evening."

Ian narrows his eyes and swivels his gaze to Denise and then back to me. "I don't know how much I like the two of you teaming up together." The amusement in his eye pushes out a little of the exhaustion and replaces it with a spark of warmth in my heart.

My weight shifts to my left foot to walk off, but instead I turn back to him and wrap him in another hug. "Darn, it's good to see you."

I meet his gaze and catch the little twinkle in his eye. Lips perked up as much as my heart is, I really do walk off this time. There's a quite warm little fire in my chest all the way home. Ian is home for a few days. And there's a load of calves for the sale Tuesday.

Maybe, just maybe Sailor will stay now.

Chapter 19

The dirty silk bookmark makes another lap around my index finger. My bottom lip begs me to stop chewing on it, but if I do I might run straight out of this quiet little church building. The verses from James three that Pastor John read aren't even the reason. It's the empty end of the pew beside me. Yesterday was such a good day, but Ian's immune system isn't up to being around all these people.

I squeezed in by the skin of my teeth as the service was starting, so I haven't had to talk to anyone. I know I'll have to, though. James already spotted me from across the aisle. I'm sure there will be a flock of others.

A rustling sound makes me look up. Pastor John is stepping off the stage drawing the fourth conclusion to his message. In a matter of moments, the piano begins to play an upbeat tune and we're standing. I close my eyes.

God put some liveliness in my veins, please.

"Thank y'all for being here. May God bless you and keep you this week. You are dismissed."

The chatter starts almost on cue, filling the building. My hands are glad to be busy putting my pen back on my notepad and stacking it on my Bible. It only takes a second, and then I'm back to figuring out what to do with myself.

Not for long though. A gentle hand touches my shoulder. "Nora, how is Ian doing? I haven't seen him or Denise lately."

And it begins. I swallow and paste on a smile. The sweet little old lady whose name I can never remember has eyebrows raised just a tick, waiting on me to get my words together.

"He's doing alright. It comes and goes. Yesterday was a good day."

She pats my arm. "Tell them we're praying for them."

"I will."

No sooner has she turned into the gentle flow of people than I sense someone over my shoulder. I turn to look up at nicely combed dark brown hair. James doesn't waste any time.

"Hey Nor, I didn't know if you'd be here this morning or not."

"Just barely." I lean against the pew. "How's that pup of yours doing?"

He switches his Bible to his other arm. "Good. He sure keeps the cows from getting too close to the pickup."

I almost spout off a teasing remark, but just as I do a man I've seen talking to Ian a dozen times appears behind James.

"Say, how's Ian doing these days? I keep meaning to give him a call, but it always ends up being late."

I put on my news bearer face and recite my standard answer again. It's all true and about all I have to offer them. I don't know any more of his treatment plan than Sailor does.

The man lifts a hand. "Glad to hear it. Tell him I said hello." Then he's walking away.

James turns to me and I feel the intensity of his gaze. He always brings out the soul-reading stare at the moments I don't need him to peer inside me.

"Thanks for moving Ian's cattle the other day. Sorry about the short notice." Maybe that'll derail his soul-reading.

He waves a hand dismissively but still eyes me. "Don't worry about it. It wasn't a big deal at all." He huffs a little laugh. "I had that pup out at the pens with me trying to get my colt trimmed when you called." He shakes his head. "Bad combo."

"Sounded like it." The scene eases my guilt about imposing on him. At least he wasn't knee deep in a crisis when I called. I stuff my free hand in my pocket and shuffle toward the side door. "Well thanks again."

"Hey Nor."

I stop just a couple steps from my exit.

"It's good to see ya."

Warmth spreads across my cheeks. "You too. Have a good week."

In the pickup, I set my Bible in the seat next to me and roll the windows down. I idle the ranch pickup to the exit of the parking lot and I look both ways. To the left to Ian's or right to my house? The hot mid-morning breeze drifts in my driver's window and out the passenger one. I flip on my blinker to the right and look for traffic. I whip out into the far lane and lean back in my seat.

At some point I have to actually do dishes and laundry. Might as well be today.

Halfway to the house my phone vibrates in my pocket. *Clay* reads across the top of the screen. My eyebrows scrunch together Clay never calls on the weekends.

My 'hello' is accompanied by a rush of wind as I get my window rolled up.

"Nora! I hope I'm not interrupting church."

"No sir, just on the way home." I let the words hang. What did he call for?

He clears his throat. "I'm going to be down in the area for some business tomorrow. What time will Ian be in Midland?"

What times do *they usually leave on Monday's?* "I think they get there about eleven in the morning. He'd be glad to see you."

"Hmm." The flapping of paper comes through the phone before his voice does. "That could work. Thank you." I don't get time to reply before his voice is jumping with business again. "Will you be around? I'll take a drive through the pastures and check cattle."

My mind fishes for what's on tomorrow's list. "As far as I know I will be."

"Good! See you then."

And before I can even start down the dirt road to the house the line is dead. I guess it is a good thing I came in case he wants to come in. At least it will be a little more presentable.

***

A dust cloud billows around the corner before the new white Chevy does. I step on the breaks and bump halfway off the road, trailer clattering.

He made it.

I give the dust a minute to settle before rolling my window down to talk to Clay.

"Found anything good back there?" He dangles his arm out the window, decked out in a crisp white shirt.

"Got a sick calf." Hanging halfway out the window, I fumble to shake his hand.

His eyebrows push at the brown felt hat on his head. "No kidding. Well let's go look at him."

"Yes sir." I suck myself back in the window. The calf's not right on the road, but that's why I have Dune. A quarter mile down the road, I pull over at the water trough and cut the engine. The cattle are scattered out in the brush a little ways off. Dune's big feet on the hardwood trailer floor echo in my ears. Hopefully the cows don't hear it, or they'll be out of there.

Dune reaches for a blade of grass while I slide into my leggins and grab the medicine out of the pickup. I slip the syringe in the pouch made of an old boot top on my saddle. One jump to catch the stirrup with my toe, and I'm in the saddle. Before Dune walks off, I adjust my leggins to be a bit more comfortable.

Clay's dust has settled, and he walks over through the prickly pear and black brush. "Got everything you need?"

"Yes, sir." *As long as they don't cross the draw before I get to him.*

Dune's head bobs, shiny mane swinging with each step. I undo the strap off my rope and start to build a loop. His ears snap to attention. Sitting deep in the saddle, I hold back the powder keg underneath me.

The cows start flicking ears nervously as soon as the first knee-high mesquite rustles. I stop the sorrel and scan the cattle. As they filter away, I spy the calf. Head drooping and a few bubbles at the mouth.

I let my hand down an inch, and Dune steps forward. My rope snags on a bush so I slip it over my shoulder. Dune starts with a lurch, crunching a couple branches. That's all it takes to get the mass of red hides running. Dune's on their tail, almost without me. He's really made a horse. I plant my butt back in the saddle and let him go.

I steady my breathing as much as I can and start to swing. One, two, three—gosh this feels awful—four five. I throw a wimpy loop six inches short of the calf. Gritting out a "damn" I coil my rope up again.

The second loop is better, and on the third time around my head I let it go. It opens up and lays over the little red and white head like it was made for it. Grabbing the slack, I jerk toward my hip and then go for the horn. With two wraps, it comes tight and swings the calf around to face us. I turn the rope over the saddle horn to hold itself. The calf lets out a half bawl.

Only then do I pay attention to where we've caught him. In the thick of a prickly pear patch. *Lovely.*

I reach behind me in the pouch for the medicine and catch a glimpse of Clay's white pickup crunching brush our way. I grimace. Those tires sure are taking a beating.

"Let me get him!" Clay hollers over the calf's bellering.

He trots across the clumps of needle grass making Dune snort and step away. I get my spur in him and he stands still long enough for me to hand the syringe down to my boss.

He holds it up to the sun then slips it in his jean pocket. "All of it?"

"Yes, sir." I lift my rein hand an inch and keep the other one on the rope as Clay goes down it. I never really thought I'd see him flank a calf like this, but I guess stranger things have happened.

The calf gives him a fight, but Clay's cowboy days come out and he has him down pretty quick. I step Dune up, and Clay throws the rope back to me.

"Need anything else with him?" He pants from where he holds the calf down.

I coil the last of my rope up, tossing a few pieces of brush back to the ground. "No, sir."

Clay lets the calf up with a pant. "Been a long time since I've done that." He hands me the syringe and starts tromping through the prickly pear back to the pickup.

I slip the syringe in my pouch as Dune starts walking off. "I appreciate your help."

"Glad I finally made it out here again. The cattle look good." He stops and watches the calf trot off bawling for momma. "Everybody's wanting me to be their lawyer lately. Makes it hard to get away."

"Yes sir." Half dry cactus petals crunch under Dune's hooves.

Clay veers around a tasahi bush and then places his hand on his pickup door handle. "What do you say we grab a bite to eat in town? Early supper, we'll go over numbers, and you can catch me up on your 'ole uncle."

I wipe the sweat out of my eyes. "Sure, sounds good."

Hopefully more talk about cattle numbers than cancer talk.

***

The music rocks along with the back and forth of the pickup cab. Supper turned out better than I thought it might. There was a whole lot more talk about cattle and the good 'ole days than the nightmare Ian's fighting right now.

One song ends, and the next gets through the first verse when I spot abandoned telephone poles in the headlights. I sit up on the edge of the seat. Ian's water lot should be right around the next corner. Things look different in the dark.

The next one really is the right corner. The H-braces become silhouettes in the beams. The headlights catch two pairs of Hereford eyes in the brush outside the water lot.

Ah, friends have come to join the captives.

Parking the pickup on the two-track road, I ease my boots to the powdery dirt. A cow pokes her head out of the brush at the same moment two others turn into the thicket.

Dang it, dang it, dang it.

I pull the half bag of cake from the bed of my pickup and rattle it. That stops them in their tracks. It also brings every last bovine already in the water lot trotting to the gate.

Goody.

A few more head come out from the brush at another rattle of the sack. There's calves, and big ones, with them. Three more shipping size calves. They'll make a full thirty-two foot trailer load with what we left up Saturday.

I perch the feed on my hip and head for the water lot gate. One handed, I wiggle the rope off and then slide back the latch. I shove the gate in, sending the cattle we left up scattering back. I slide the sack down my arm so cubes start falling out, and take off at a brisk walk.

Sack empty, I ease around the fence toward the gate. I'm a couple yards away from it when the last calf darts in to start eating. *Score.*

I stretch each stride as far as my legs will let me, picking up the pace without scattering the herd out the gate. I have it halfway closed when a cow throws her head up and whirls, but I'm too far ahead of her. When she realizes the gap isn't open, she runs herself up between two peacefully eating cows.

I slide the one-inch pipe latch into the wallowed-out hole in the cross tie post and reach for the string that was tied around it. My phone rings in my pocket. Pulling it out, I read a name with *Horse Club* under it. I slide the green circle and raise it to my ear. "Hello."

"Hello, this is George. Mindi's husband."

Oh, George. I hadn't even paid attention to who from the horse club was calling. "Yes sir?"

"The cattle we had lined up for the next sorting aren't going to end up working out, and your name was brought up."

My name? For what? Clay's cattle? I lean against the gate and squint off at the horizon even though it's darn near dark.

"Yes, sir." I nudge a stick around with the toe of my boot. "Uh, we don't have any yearlings or anything right now."

"Right, right. Okay. Do you know of anyone else that might have some replacement heifers maybe?"

The feed sack rattles under my arm. "Uh, let me think." Ian's are a little small, besides they're going to the sale in the morning.

I crumple up the sack and start for the pickup. *Wade's cattle.* If James has enough replacement heifers that aren't bred yet, I bet he wouldn't mind.

"James Butler, I think he said he made it to the last sorting. He might have some yearling heifers that you could use." I stuff the sack behind the toolbox and slide in the cab.

"Alright. Do you have his phone number?"

I yank the pickup door closed. "Yes sir. I'll text it to you if that'll work."

"That'll be great. Thank you!"

I put the pickup in gear and ease off the brake. "Yes sir."

"Have a good evening. M'bye." The line beeps three times.

A bump rattles the trailer, and I shake my head. Never thought I'd be the one connecting people. I barely knew ten people this time last year.

I text James's number to George and then shoot James a message too. At least that way he'll know how they got around to asking him.

I make it around to the pens at the house and peek in on Tripod, his momma, and the bull. They're all alive and Tripod's splint is still on. *That's a miracle.*

***

A hoot owl puts out a rhythmic set of calls as I saddle Dune in the dim light of the barn. Cinches done, I hang his bridle around the saddle horn and look up at the trees, searching for the owl's silhouette.

I lead Dune to the trailer. The gate latch squeaks and then is replaced by the clomp of his big feet on the wood floor boards. It's time to load us some calves and get to the sale.

Headlights lighting up the black top and Ryan Fritz jingling the horses in on the radio, I soak in the morning. I actually have the time to. No crisis for me to get to as soon as I get this done.

Turning off on the dirt road into Ian's pasture, I roll the window down and pull my jacket collar up against the breeze. Around the bend, the outside posts of the water lot stick out of the low brush. I drum my fingers on the top of the steering wheel. Getting these calves sold will take a boulder of a load off of Ian.

I start looking for the bald white faces of the Herefords. My eyes can't find them. They're probably just laid up by the fence. Coming up next to the lot my heart stops. It's empty.

Several seconds I sit there with my foot on the brake and will the cattle to appear. Finally I drag in a breath and kick the Chevy out of gear. I put the emergency brake on and push the door open.

The gate is laid a couple feet open with a beat-out trail between it and the post. What I did hits me upside the head. *I didn't tie the gate last night.* I had been on the phone and didn't even think of it.

I poke my head in the cab and flip my phone over for the time. *7:30.* It'll take an act of Congress to get any of them much less the whole trailer load of them back in this lot. If I did manage to get that done, the sale would be over by the time I get them to town.

I shake my head. *There's no way.*

Stomach churning, I pick up my phone. I center in on Ian's name the second I open the call app. Those calves were going to sell really well this week. He'd studied the market seven ways from Sunday.

I swallow the lump of guilt, but then it just stirs up the fight that's already happening in my gut. My fingers curl around the phone in my hand. *Stupid thing.* If I hadn't of answered it last night the freaking cattle would still be here.

I chuck the phone in the passenger seat. It bounces up and then into the floorboard. *Good.*

Since when did I start thinking I can do more than one thing at a time? I barely managed to finish calving the heifers and hunt for a new lease last spring.

Leaning across the seat, I finger the phone closer until I can wrap my fingers around it. Bile rises up in my throat as I open it and tap on Ian's contact.

It rings four times before his muffled voice says, "Hello."

"Hey…" I drag the word out a little as if the longer I take to get the words out the easier it will get. "I didn't get the gate tied last night and the cattle got out of the water lot. I can try to get them up and sorted, but I think it'll be too late to get them to the sale barn. I'm sorry."

A low heavy sigh. "Nah, that's alright, girl. We'll get them next week."

"Okay." I pick at a nick in the steering wheel. "I'm sorry."

"It's alright. I never did get around to welding that gate so that they can't do that. Next week will work just as well."

I'm sorry is the only thing that will come to mind, but I don't want to be a broken record. If he could see my face I'd just nod. I grapple to find a word to say.

"Well, girl, I got some medicine to take, so I'll holler at you later."

I didn't think my heart could ache any more, but the abruptness of the end of the call adds a pang. "Sounds good." The words come out weakly.

The call goes dead, and I let my phone fall to the seat cushions. I lean my head back and rake my hands down my face. *Of all the things to screw up.*

I plop my hat back on my head, and put the pickup in drive. The one thing he's asked of me. *One thing.* And I can't even get that done.

Chapter 20

Back and forth, Cante's head swings as his strides stretch out long and swift. Two washed out red cows, calves in tow, keep themselves in front of us. They're lined out on the fence line like they know they're headed for home.

A breeze blows, and I pull my jacket collar up higher. After yesterday's high in the nineties, today's seventy degrees, drizzling, and breezy is making me want to go pull out the full on coats.

I duck my head so my hat cuts the wind from my face. That's less about the temperature and more about how dried-out my eyes are. I close them for a second. Poor things emptied every ounce of moisture on my pillow last night.

It just shouldn't be this way—Ian, the calves, any of it.

A check for those calves should be going in the mail to Ian today. Instead I'm zoning out trailing cattle while Ian's getting Vitamin C pumped into his veins.

Thankfully these neighbor cattle are pretty nice. They don't always respect a patch in the fence, but they honor a horse, unlike the cattle neighboring the other side of the ranch. I shake my head. Dune or Banks would have had to make the circle this morning if those were the neighbor cows over here. Cante doesn't read a cow quite that well yet.

I tuck the tips of my fingers in the pocket on my leggins just in time to feel my phone vibrating farther down in it. First time it has rang this morning. It's been nice.

The screen is too dark for me to read the name across the top. I slide at the bottom of the phone and put it to my ear. "Hello?"

"Hey, Nor, what you up to?"

James. I hesitate. How much do I tell him this time?

"Just trailing a couple of the neighbors' cows up to the pens." I rest one hand on the saddle horn and relax back in the saddle. "You?"

"Well darn, that's way more fun." He mumbles something under his breath. "I'm headed to town to load up this trailer with feed."

My eyebrows crinkle together. "You're not getting it at Sam's?"

"Yeah, I am."

I cock my head. Wade always got the overhead bin filled up, but I guess things change. "Oh, gotcha."

"Dadgummit." The word comes through the phone like the far off beller of a mad bull.

One side of my mouth quirks up. "You good?"

"Feed sacks keep flying out. I thought I'd stuffed them all in the toolbox at the cattle guard." Plastic crunches drowning out his words. "Anyway, what are you doing this weekend?"

That's three days away, I don't have a clue what crisis will come up between now and then. "Uh, I got to get Ian's calves up and to the sale barn Monday."

"That's not the weekend."

My eyes roll up into my head before the last of the words are out of his mouth. *Thanks, Mr. Obvious.* "I don't know, fixing whatever falls apart between now and then, I guess."

"Why don't you take some cows to the sale with me?"

Cante drifts off to the right, making me look up and actually halfway pay attention. The cows have wandered off the fence a couple yards to another trail. "When?"

"Saturday."

I roll my bottom lip in between my teeth. Seeing some different country does sound pretty nice. If these cattle respect the patch I put in the draw I could probably manage a day. But Ian...

I guess I take too long mulling it over, because James asks, "What else do you have that you need to do this week?"

Squinting, I draw up my mental image of each pasture. "Cake these cows here at the house. They're probably out of syrup back in the Bowler pasture." *And not screw up things for Ian again.*

"I can come over and help you tomorrow."

The edge of my lips perk up. "Don't you have cattle of your own to take care of?"

His low chuckle vibrates through the phone line. "Don't you worry about my cows. I've got them tended to just fine."

I laugh a little. I'm sure he does. When it comes to cattle, James doesn't miss much. "Where is it again that you're trying to drag me off to?"

"I'm not dragging you anywhere." His eye roll carries through his voice. "I'm *inviting* you to haul some cows to San Saba with me."

"An invitation, how official." I can't help giving him a little crap. He doesn't reciprocate though, so I get a little more serious. "Why's Wade sending them out there?"

A flat sigh. "Nor."

A little grin parts my lips. I really wasn't trying to get under his skin this time.

"Do you want to go, or not?"

I scratch at a knick in the saddle horn. Before I even open my mouth I know my words are going to come out with the confidence of a rabbit poking out the end of a pipe. "Will you help me pen Ian's cows Monday?"

"You bet." His voice is sure and strong, any irritation gone.

My shoulders drop. "Thank you." *But is getting the calves to the sale enough?*

"I'll be by about six Saturday morning?" He leaves the words hanging with a question mark.

For a second I wonder what he'd say if I said no, but I've given him enough crap for one phone call. "Sounds good."

The conversation over, I slip the phone back into my leggins pocket. I tuck the ends of my fingers in the pocket too, but just for a second. Then I'm fishing my phone out again and finding Ian's contact. I hit call.

It rings four or five times before he answers. "Hey girl." It's *almost* his normal greeting.

"Hey, how's it going?"

Some rustling comes through the phone. "D agreed I've earned myself a burger for lunch, so it's not too bad." With the teasing in his voice, I figure Denise is within earshot.

"There you go. Sounds like a good deal." I adjust my reins in my hand. "Be sure to find you one of them fancy ones."

His deep laugh fills up the speaker. "Put some bacon and green chiles on it. Good stuff."

My eyelids sink closed for a moment. *Man, it's good to hear some strength and excitement in his voice.*

"What's on your mind?"

I sit up straight. My mouth has suddenly gone dry. Just having a burger makes his day, and I want to leave the country for a whole day. "Well, I was going to see what you had in mind for the weekend."

"Ah, not a whole lot right now. What are you thinking?"

"Uh, well, James wants me to go with him to haul some cows on Saturday."

"James, huh?" I can hear the quirk of his eyebrows through his voice.

Heat rushes across my cheeks. "It's just Saturday, and then he's going to help me gather up those calves on Monday."

"Shoot, girl, go for it. You kids have fun."

I smile sheepishly. "Are you sure you don't need anything? We can pick something up if you needed—"

"Y'all just have a good time."

"Thanks," I murmur, bumping Cante back into the trail.

"I'm going to go find that burger. I'll holler at you later this evening."

I sit deeper in the warm leather saddle and let it wrap me in a hug. "Alright. Enjoy it."

Looking up to really pay attention to the cows, I let a whole cheesy smile bloom on my face. All day in the pickup with James, I might find enough to give him a hard time about. Pay back for all the crap he's dealt me.

I jiggle the reins. Cante's head perks up a bit, and I smooch him up to push the cows back to the fence. They drift back like trail broke steers, and we go back to plodding along. By the time the pens come into view I've worked myself from excited to nervous.

Cante's long trot carries us in a circle around the cows and up to the gate. I lean over, halfway out of the saddle to undo the chain latch. The gate squeaks open, and we trot back out. The cows have stopped in the trail and only pick up their slow walk when Cante is breathing down their tails.

Gate closed behind them, I point Cante back into the pasture where we left the pickup. *That was a pretty good morning's job, if I say so myself.*

Chapter 21

My hairbrush hangs up on a knot in my hair as I drag it through. The wind while I was putting molasses out sure did a number on my hair.

I toss the brush on the counter and divide my hair into three parts. Fingers grasping the auburn strands, I start braiding them together. I'm just wrapping a hair band around the end of the braid when the rattle of a trailer shakes to a halt. Perfect timing.

I gulp the last lukewarm swallow of coffee, set the cup in the sink, and wipe my mouth with the towel on the counter. My wallet barely fits in the tiny front pocket on the one pair of jeans that haven't been abused yet. I slide my phone in my back pocket as boot heels thud on the porch.

My fingers intertwine with themselves as I hover a few feet from the door. Do I open the it? Or let him knock? Before I can answer myself there is a light tap.

I lick my lips and reach for the door knob. The hinges creak and I cringe. "Good morning."

"Morning." He tucks the tips of his fingers in his pockets and sweeps the for-once clean kitchen with his gaze.

I set my felt hat firmly on my head. Out of the corner of my eye I catch on of his eyebrows raising. "I can look at least half presentable."

He rolls his eyes as he puts a hand on the warped wooden door. "You always look presentable."

My neck catches fire. "Thanks."

The pickup cab is freezing, with dang near ice particles flying out of the vents. I thought the mornings had started to cool off, but I guess not for Polar Bear James. I tuck myself into the passenger seat. James closes my door softly.

I start forming my list of things to bring up. Topics that don't end up with being sad and tired.

The driver's door slams, and James's shining bright teeth flash over at me. I don't know how the well water hasn't stained them yet. "Isn't it a fine morning?"

I relax against the console at his upbeat tone. "What's got you in such a chipper mood?"

The diesel engine growls low and steady as we pull away from the house. "These cows ought to bring a decent price, and I ain't got to make this long drive by myself. What more can I ask for?"

Ian to be in his office or on Sailor.

The thought takes over my mind without permission, dropping the smile from my face. I swallow back the salty tears that threaten to spill over.

That's what I would ask for.

On the highway, the engine groans to get up to speed. It chugs along a little bit before James punches buttons on the steering wheel. He props his left wrist on the top of the wheel and bends his right knee. One look my direction from him sends me scrambling for something to talk about. James is just enough like Ian that he'll do some of that slap the console and grin stuff. It's a little early in the trip for that.

"How's your colt coming along?" *There, a good topic to start off with. It ought to be pretty safe.*

"Ah, he's coming along." James flips on his blinker and get over in the passing lane. "I get caught up in other stuff and haven't stayed with him very consistently. But he's doing real well."

I lay the seat back a notch and rest my hat on my knee. "Where'd you get him from?"

He looks at me long enough that I catch the sparkle of amusement in his eyes. "Off my dad. He picked him up in Alpine. A quarter draft, so he ought to grow into the big 'ole feet he's got on him."

"Nice."

We discuss one horse topic and then another until the conversation lulls. I stare out the window, watching mesquites fade into cedar. The country whirls by fast enough I only get about half of it looked over before it's gone.

The full bar ditches we pass remind me of a drive with Ian. We'd gone east to Mr. Wellman's place. But that was back in the day before the land burned and took several people's plans with it—mine being one of them.

I wonder how Mr. Wellman's doing these days.

Several minutes slip by. Finally, James rests his elbow on the console and groans with a stretch of his neck. "What do you want for lunch?"

I shrug my shoulders. "I don't care. Just not seafood."

"I can do that." Between glances to the road, he scrolls on his phone for a minute. "Looks like there's Mexican food or Whataburger."

"Okay."

His narrowed eyes draw a little grin to my face. Food decisions are one thing I'm sure I'll outlast him on. He likes to eat too much to force me into deciding.

"Looks like Whataburger has plenty of room to get in and out of. You good with that?"

My grin blooms. I knew he'd get around to making up his mind. "Sounds good."

***

White and orange lined paper bags crinkle on the console. I hand James his burger as he guides the rig around a corner out of town. Unwrinkling the paper from around my burger with pickles only, I watch the buildings fade away out the window. For once my mind stops racing.

Halfway through the carton of fries, James's voice draws me back to the real world. "Hey Nor." His voice is softer than normal, splitting the steady hum of the engine like a knife through warm butter.

I look over from staring out the window. "Yeah?"

"Are you doing okay?" He pauses. "Is something wrong? I mean more than what Ian has going on?" A truck passes us, drawing James's attention.

I stop fiddling with a piece of hay I fished from the seat crevice. Staring at it, I try to remember every time I've been around him lately. What did I say that he might be referring to? "No. Things have been busy, but that's all."

He stares straight ahead.

I start running the hay underneath my thumb nail. "Why do you ask?"

A muscle on his jaw line twitches. He puts his right hand on the steering wheel, too. A big truck creeps by us. "I thought we were friends, Nora."

Thought we *were?* We aren't? I swallow. "Me too."

The bumpy road allows him only a second's glance in my direction. "Really? Is that why you'll answer my calls and go out to eat with me a couple days and then ignore my pitiful messages for you to just tell me you're still alive?" His hands grip the steering wheel tight enough to strain the skin of his hand.

That sparks the mound of frustration that's been building since that C word came into our lives. "I've been busy. By the time I get home at night I'm doing good if I remember to eat, let alone respond to messages. Not to mention the twenty people that think they need updates on Ian every other day."

I've been trying to do *enough*.

His head is already shaking back and forth before the words even get all the way out of my mouth. "No, Nor, don't give me that. There's more to it."

What does he want me to say? I drive my finger nail through the middle of the sprig of hay. A growl pushes its way out between my lips. If he knows so he ought to know that it's a touch more than work that's keeping me from answering the phone.

That invisible hand that grabs my throat all too often is at it again. I swallow, but it only grips tighter. My eyes sting.

The tick of the blinker fills the silence of the cab. I heave in air to try and drive out the tears. I look out the window. *Just trying to stay afloat—that's all I've been doing.* I've dropped a lot of balls. I know I have.

I remember April's eyes when Charlie left her in the dirt. She deserves better.

"We missed you at the playday Saturday."

I shake my head.

"They got out last night."

"Don't worry about it, girl."

The pickup slows to a crawl. My shoulders jump with one silent graspy sob. There's rustling across the pickup cab, but I don't look over as James steps out.

At least April and the others at the horse club have other people that stepped up. But Ian… I squeeze my eyes shut. The image of his ghostly face under his hat brim won't leave. There's no one to blame for dropping the ball on those calves, but me.

Sale-barn air reminds me why we're here. One thought rings through my head as I push the door open.

I've failed Ian. I've failed him big.

Chapter 22

The sale barn man's voice blurs together with James's. Another gaspy sob threatens to explode out of me. I reach for the trailer and glance through the bars at James on the other side.

I hurt him too—along with everyone else.

The trailer gate squeaks. Three cows step off, and then I release the partition gate. Four more sets of hooves rock the trailer as they step off. One more gate swings open, four more cows walk off the trailer. James and the sale barn man follow them through the maze of gates and fences.

Stepping in the trailer to pin back the partition gates, I shake my head. *Lord, only you know why Jame is hard headed enough to keep pestering me.*

I slide the last latch into place and turn up the side of the trailer. I'm in the passenger seat all of thirty seconds before James slides in the driver's side. He tucks a paper in the console and then we're off.

I drag in a breath. Sparing a sideways flick of my eyes, I make a moment's eye contact with James. "I'm sorry."

"I'm sorry for bouncing back and forth and blowing you off." My mouse-ish words are barely loud enough to make it over the diesel's pur.

James turns onto the highway and then props his elbow on the console.

"I hadn't even realized what I've been doing." I lace my fingers together in my lap. "But doesn't make it okay. I've just been trying to keep all the irons in the pot. Whether they get hot or not, at least they stay in the pot."

Saying that out loud sounds really stupid.

Seconds slug by with no response from him. Finally, he drags a hand across his clean shaven chin. "You don't have to be the only one keeping the irons hot."

I draw a knee up to my chest. Such an Ian thing to say. It makes my heart smile a little in a bittersweet kind of way.

Again a couple more seconds pass. I wet my lips. "I've let a lot of people down lately. Including you. I'm sorry."

James squeezes my shoulder with his free hand. "It's okay." His voice is thick.

My cheeks warm as his hand lingers on my shoulder. *It's really not.* I'm hugging my knee to my chest when a loud pop startles us both. James's hand flies to the wheel and he leans up to study through the mirror.

"Running empty," he mutters, pushing the button for the flashers. The engine gears down and he guides the pickup to a clear spot on the side of the road.

In unison, we throw open our doors and hop to the ground. He pulls a case of sockets and an impact wrench from the back seat. I jump up in the bed of the pickup for the wooden wedge. I slide it in front of the front trailer tire.

James rounds the end of the trailer with the tools.

"You want to pull up on this block?"

"Yes ma'am." He lays the cases on the trailer fender and disappears again.

The trailer rolls up just enough that the front tire sits squarely on the block. I make an educated guess and manage to get the right size socket to fit. I put it on the impact wrench and start it whirling the lug nuts off.

IN BETWEEN PASTURES

James's long frame hops up on the bed of the pickup. He hoists the spare off its perch on the trailer neck.

The lug nuts off, I rock the tire back and forth until it sits on the ground.

James rolls the spare tire up, clearing his throat. "I'll finish."

Standing from a squat, I give him a stare. "I can do it."

"I'm well aware of what you *can* do. Doesn't mean you have to." He puts one hand on the blown out tire and rolls it out of the way. "Let me."

I step out of his way. "If it makes you happy."

He slips the spare tire on the bolts in a flash and starts running the lug nuts on. While he does, I roll the ruined tire to the pickup bed.

"Don't—"

I heave it onto the bed of the pickup while the impact wrench whirls its tune in James's hand. Taking a pickin' string from the headache rack, I run it through the rim and tie it in.

He puts the socket and wrench in their cases. His lips quirk to one side. "You sure make it hard to be a gentleman."

"Sorry." I giggle and wait for him to back off the block. When it's free I pick it up and wedge it back in its place on the pickup bed.

I settle back into the seat and the wheels start turning again.

The pickup changes gears a couple times getting up to speed, and then James props up on the console. "Well that was fun."

"It's amazing we made it this far before that happened."

He punches buttons to set the cruise. "That's for sure."

A few moments pass; I stare out the window and watch the world go by. A little green reflective toothpick of a sign comes and goes by the window.

"Twenty-four miles to Eden." James flips on his blinker to pass a blue Volkswagen. "I bet they have a tire shop. You want to look it up and find out?"

I lift my phone, unlock it, and tap the compass. Immediately a black screen with little gray words pops up. "I don't have service."

James lifts up his phone. "Huh, neither do I." He puts the device back in the cup holder and shrugs a shoulder. "We'll find out if they have one when we get to town I guess."

With the trailer empty, James runs a little faster than on the way down. It doesn't take long before the speed limit drops and buildings start clustering around one another. We stop at the red light. A mural of Adam and Eve stretches above us outside my window, inspired by the town's name: Eden. It's nice art, but I squirm at their giant eyes on me.

I pick up my phone again, but still no service. *Weird*.

James checks his too. "Tell me when the light's green." He taps around on his device, so evidently he has service.

A few seconds pass. "It's green."

He flips on his right blinker and eases on the gas pedal. "There's one a couple blocks down."

The trailer bounces in a pothole at the next stop sign. We pass through a block of crummy houses before James pulls up on the side of a cinder block building with a green paint job that never got finished.

James does the talking to people while I climb up in the nose of the trailer and pull out a good tire. I roll it out the side door of the trailer. After leaning it up against the pickup bed, I untie the ruined tire from the front of the bed.

"I'll get it." The voice comes out of nowhere.

My heart turns into a cottontail rabbit, stopping for half a second and then taking off at top speed. *Lord have mercy where did he come from?*

A skinny bean pole of a kid reaches for the tire as I step away. In the spots on his arms that aren't covered in black tire smudges, his skin glows almost as white as mine. That's an accomplishment. Rarely do I meet people as white as I am.

The kid takes the good tire from James and wheels one with each hand into the shop.

"You get service?"

I shake my head. "I didn't when we pulled up anyway." I fetch my phone from the pickup. Still nothing. I hold down a button on each side until it starts powering off. I lean back up against the pickup beside James and slip the device in my pocket.

"What do you think?"

I draw a smiley face on the pickup bed. If his voice wasn't so different, I'd think I was standing beside Ian. I let out a heavy breath and slowly bring my head up so that I can glance at James from under my hat brim. "I try to do as little of that as possible."

His eyebrows arch. "I don't know how much I believe that."

"You should believe it a lot." My lips quirk a smile and I go back to drawing in the dust on the flatbed. "What do *you* think?"

"Ah, I'm thinking I'm about due for a nap."

A bubble of laughter comes out just short of a snort. "You sound more and more like a crippled up old man."

"Thank you—" his voice trails off as he pulls his phone from his pocket. "I appreciate that."

His eyebrows are scrunched together as he lifts the device to his ear and says a firm "Hello." He stands straight from his reclined position against the pickup cab.

I move to a fresh spot of dust and start to write my name.

"Yes ma'am, here she is." He bumps my shoulder. Jerking up, my hand hits his. "It's Denise."

My heart doesn't stop this time before it runs off. Denise? I didn't even know she had James's number. What happened? "Hello?" My voice is shaky.

"Nora, I'm so sorry to bother you."

I swallow a cotton ball that has taken up residence in my mouth. "Don't be. What's going on?" My hands turn cold even though the sun is shining bright.

A quaking breath muffles through the phone line for a moment. "Ian's in the hospital. His fever spiked and he was throwing up blood. They air-flighted him out of the hospital in town. We're in Lubbock now."

Hospital. Air-flight. Lubbock. The words whirl and crash together. My throat hugs itself, making it hard for the little air my lungs shoves out to actually leave my body.

"Wh—what do you need?"

"They've got him on IV antibiotics, and that's brought his fever down. That's all I know for sure."

I run a hand down my face. A strong arm grips my shoulders and I lean into it. My legs are wobbly posts. *Lubbock, Texas and I'm way the hell out here.* I want to stomp and yell, but all that my body will do is wilt.

"I'll be up there as soon as I can be. Do you need stuff from the house? What can I bring you?"

I hear muffled background voices. "I'll text you a few things. The nurse just came in."

The phone beeps, and my arm slowly pulls it away from my face. "Bye," I whisper.

My eyes are open, but I see nothing. There are noises, but all I can hear are my own thoughts stuck in one loop. *Hospital. Air-flight. Lubbock.* I can't seem to get past those three words.

God, this can't be happening.

A sob comes from such a deep place it shakes my whole chest. My hat leaves my head, and then I'm burying my face in James' vest.

I don't know how long I water his vest with my tears. Just as I've about run out of tears, I hear voices and feel James's arms loosen around me.

"Hey, Nor, give me just a second, I got to get my wallet."

I step back from him, keeping my back to the tire guy. I don't need to look in a mirror to know my face is a scary sight.

The gate latch on the trailer squeaks, more voices, and then it squeaks again. "Thank you!" James's voice is loud, right beside me, and then his arm is around my shoulders again.

I wipe at my eyes.

"What happened, Nor? What did she say?"

A stray sob makes me gasp for air. I wipe my eyes with the cuff of my shirt and pull in a long breath. Poor James. Just holding me while I irrigate his vest, and he doesn't even know why.

I swallow. "Ian's in the hospital in Lubbock. They air-flighted him there."

James sucks in air. "Is he alright? I, uh, I mean—"

"They have him on antibiotics that brought his fever down." I wipe snot a little farther up my shirt sleeve.

"Can we go to the house?" I choke the words out just before more tears start falling down my cheeks.

He wraps both his arms around me, sure and strong. I cling to him, chest heaving with sobs.

"Yes." His voice shudders.

In a few moments he lets one arm drop from around me. I do the same and let that hand wipe at my eyes again. His arm is firmly around my shoulders, guiding me around the front of the pickup. It's a good thing too, because our feet are a blurry sight through my eyes.

I manage to get in the seat even through the lack of brain function I have.

"Why don't you drink a little of that?" James holds up my half gallon water jug.

I reach for it. Tears claw up my throat again as I rub my finger over the 'Nora' Ian carved in the side of it. *I'm not losing him.* I tell myself that, but I don't know how much I believe it.

James's voice interrupts my thoughts. "Good to go?"

No. But I nod. "Thank you."

He closes the door and in a moment is in the driver's seat. He slides my hat on the dash—the hat that I kinda forgot I even had on today. "Do we need to go to your house, or up there, or?"

"Home. Or to Ian's. Denise is going to text me some stuff to bring to them."

"Okay."

The wheels start turning. I wipe my eyes again with the bit of my shirt sleeve that isn't soaked.

"I'm sorry." It comes out just above a whisper.

His hand rests next to mine. "Don't apologize."

I slip my hand in his and lean back against the seat. "I don't think this is how you imagined today going." I glance over to watch the briefest smile pass across his face before he squeezes my hand.

"Well, no, that phone call wasn't part of the plan, but I really just wanted to spend time with you." A little color touches his cheeks. He spares a glance from the road. "To put a smile on your face."

Those words do just that. It's a sad smile, but one nonetheless.

Chapter 23

The oil field supply sign sticks up like a toothpick in a sandwich, announcing town. I smooth my hair down and then plunk my hat on top of it.

"Your house, or Ian's?"

"Ian's." I scroll through Denise's texts and build a list in my head.

Get Ian's bag, fix one for Denise, grab her list of things from the pantry, and make a run by the dogs and the cattle up in the pens.

James goes straight through the yellow light, stays in the left lane, and mashes on the gas pedal. When the dirt road to their house comes up, the brakes squeal as he makes the turn

As soon as the pickup stops in front of the house, I bust the pickup door open and zip to Ian's jiggly back door. First stop, the bathroom. When I come out, I start for the pantry.

"What can I do?"

I stop. Looking up from the list Denise texted me, it takes a second before I have an answer. "The dogs are all in their pens. They need two scoops of food and top off their water."

"Yes ma'am." His footsteps clomp out the door.

I grab a plastic bag from the wad hanging in the pantry and start shoving things in it. A bag of cashews is nearly full and stretched the bag a little by the time everything else is in there too. I slip another bag around it, tie the tops, and leave it on the kitchen counter.

Onto the next thing.

I stride to the big wooden door that leads to Ian and Denise's bedroom. She told me to go in here to get things. It still feels weird though. I stand in front of it a moment before I ease the handle down and take a revenant step inside.

A big painting hangs over the bed. A little brown headed girl atop a bay horse and her leggin clad daddy leaned up against the horse talking to her. He's got a grin on his face and if his eyes were part of the picture they'd be glowing.

I swallow. *Ian and Kayla.*

The click of a closing door puts my feet to moving and I drag my gaze away from the painting. I didn't think my chest could ache anymore than it did when I walked in this house—turns out it can.

I gather the things from the bathroom Denise asked for. A sweep around the bathroom and a peek in the closet turn up empty for Ian's bag. I pull out my phone again and scroll through her text until I find the part about the bag.

At the end of the bed.

I turn around to face the big metal frame. If it was a snake it would have bit me. A bag in each hand I take one more long look at the painting. My throat closes up.

Selfishly, God, please don't let them meet again yet.

"Nor?"

I swallow, turn, and pull the door back closed behind me. "Yeah." I round the corner and almost run into James.

"Hey, the dogs are tended to. Everything up in the pens will be good for a couple days. What else do you need?"

The painting is still burning a hole in my mind. I could get a lot more done if it wasn't.

"Nor? You okay?" One of his hands rests on my shoulder. The other takes the first one and then the other bag from my hand. "What is it?"

I bite the inside of my lip. A shuddering breath leaves my throat before I force my eyes up to James's. "I can't lose him. I'm not ready."

For the third time in a matter of hours, I'm wrapped in his strong arms, face pressed up against his chest.

"You're not losing him. Not right now."

I take in a slow, long breath. One that smells of hay dust, french fries, and men's shampoo. How can he be so sure? I want to be sure, but I'm also sure that God's plan ain't the same as mine.

A few moments pass and then I pull back from James' arms. "Better get on the road." I pick up a bag, but James gets the other before I can pick it up too. He stands behind me ready to move at the word. "You don't have to—"

He starts shaking his head. "You ain't driving up there by yourself." A little grin quirks one side of his lips. "Besides, you rode here with me and your house is out of the way."

My lips twitch up on one side. "As long as you don't mind."

"Not even a little bit." The words are low as he reaches for the bag in my hand. I let him take it.

Getting the plastic bag off the counter, I flip off the kitchen light and whisper, "They'll be back."

Turning out the door, the urgency to know for myself that Ian's okay takes root in my chest. James has the pickup running, lights on, and trailer unhooked. He thought of things I wouldn't have.

I hop back in the cab, set the bag in the backseat and melt against the cushion. The slow soft tune through the radio makes it easier to relax. "You can bend him, but you can't break him. It takes years of work and dirt and hurt to make him. But when the whole world falls apart he'll hold together." The song plays just loud enough I can make out the words.

James' hand appears palm up on the console. His eyes stay trained straight ahead on the road. Another line of the song plays through the radio.

My elbow rests on the very edge of the console. I pull my bottom lip in between my teeth. Slowly, I slip my hand in his. I'm glad he doesn't mind hauling me all over the country. I don't want to drive up to that hospital by myself.

It's pitch black except for the street lights when James backs into a parking spot between two sports cars. He rolls down the window to pull his mirror in. I pull the one on my side in too.

James takes the two big bags, and I get the little one. We strike out for the big building at a walk just fast enough to not be piddling. My adrenaline has been replaced by dread of what I don't want to see.

Following the directions Denise outlined in a text, we trek down a hall, around the corner, up the elevator and land in an octagon of a waiting room. I let out a big breath; it doesn't relieve the pressure in my chest though.

In a chair in the corner I set the bag down. I send Denise a text that we're here and then turn to James. I press my lips into a thin line and type my fingers on the back of my phone. My phone dings and in a few moments, Denise appears behind a big wooden door.

A hint of red lines her eyes and her voice is a little strained when she says, "Thank y'all so much for coming."

I swallow and wrap her in a hug, as much for me as for her. "How are you?"

She nods and wipes under her eyes. "Alright. They're taking good care of him." She nods again and takes a big breath. Turning, she gives James a hug too.

"Do you want to sit?" James offers.

Denise takes the chair at the end of a row. James looks at me, but I shake my head. I've sat all day and my nerves are having a race around my body.

Denise shakes her head. "He got Sailor up and rode. I didn't think it was a good idea, but I've stopped telling him what I think unless he asks for it."

My heart drops to my toes, flies through my stomach, and gets stuck in my throat. Riding Sailor. He's so weak. He was weak last week, who knows what another seven days of treatment and fighting has done. "Why'd they fly him from town?"

"Because of the GI bleed. They can't do anything for it at that small of a hospital."

Flying still seems a bit excessive for no more rowled up than they are about it here. But I'm not a doctor.

"The doctors said riding wasn't the cause. The infection around the stint and the energy it took to ride just tipped the scale. But they've got his fever down from this morning, so it seems like they have the right antibiotic for the infection."

I swallow. *Can't they just fix it?* But I know they can't. It doesn't work like that.

Riding Sailor. What was he thinking? What was he trying to do? If I would have been there I could have done it for him.

A tender hand rests on my shoulder. "Why don't you go see him? It's room three-twelve."

I look up at Denise. Worry lines are sunk deep into her forehead. Her eyes hang tired. I nod. "Thanks." It takes a couple seconds before my feet agree to carry me to the room.

A glance over my shoulder and I catch a thin smile from James. "I'll be waiting out here," he says just loud enough I can hear him.

I push the button on the wall for the doors into the hallway. The nurse doesn't even ask who I'm there for, just says it's open. I figured this late at night they'd be picky. The door is heavy as I push it open enough to slip through.

312. The numbers jump off of the plate beside the door. I take in a steadying breath. It stops my heart altogether. The handle is cold under my sweaty palm. It takes a couple seconds before I can convince my hand to actually push it down.

The door doesn't make a sound as I push it back a couple feet. I slip through and take a quiet step to see around the corner where the bed is. A ghost of a legend is covered up with a pale green blanket. His head is turned away from the door, but I can still see that his eyes are closed. The heels of my boots don't do a very good job of being quiet as I edge closer to the bed.

Tears climb my throat. I don't try to push them back. "I'm sorry." I reach out to touch his skeleton of a hand, but draw back. "I'm so sorry."

I'm sorry I let you down. I'm sorry you're laying in this bed right now.

Beside the plastic railed hospital bed an IV pole holds up three bags. An oxygen tube sits above his drawn cheeks, pumping air into his nostrils. Silent tears run down my cheeks.

I'm sorry that I went off galavanting around the country and left you to feel like you had to do it yourself. I'm sorry you're not strong enough to do it and have a bang up story to tell.

My shoulders shudder with a sob. "One that doesn't end with you here."

Chapter 24

A clock at the end of the hospital hallway reads *11:08* as I step out of Ian's room. Apparently the charge nurse tonight doesn't care about visiting hours.

I walk as fast as my legs will go without breaking into a full-blown trot. Denise and James stroll just ahead, shoes squeaking against the shiny tile floor. A few more strides and James looks over his shoulder. He stops and I'm glad. My lungs aren't used to breathing sterilized air that fast, and the fluorescent lights blare into my eyes.

"Hey," he drawls.

"Hey." I step closer to them as a nurse's aid passes with a squeaky-wheeled cart. I turn to Denise. "How much did Ian settle on for Sailor?"

She wraps her sweater tighter around her. "I don't know, I think ten thousand, maybe?"

He's worth it. It might be a stretch to squeeze that, but it'll happen. I flip my gaze to James. "Is your pickup unlocked?"

He starts fishing in his pocket. "No, but here's the keys. Where you going?"

"You're not driving home tonight are you?" Denise looks between the two of us.

My mind is far from home. "I'm just going to make a phone call."

James matches me for a few speedy strides. "Be careful."

"I will. I'll be back in a few minutes." I jump on the elevator as a nurse is getting off and hit the button for the main floor.

Leaning against the flatbed of James's pickup, I let out the first good breath I've taken in a while. I find Mindi's contact and hit call. Nevermind the fact that she's probably already headed for bed.

The night breeze rustles the tree James parked under. I rub my right arm that is holding up my phone. I almost want to snuggle into the passenger seat, but breathing real air is too refreshing for that. The phone rings about five times and then a half awake "hello" comes through the line.

"Hey Mindi, sorry it's late."

Her voice is groggy as she says, "That's alright. Is everything okay?"

My thumb nail drags along my index finger. I've gotten to know Mindi pretty well the last year or so, but this is a little out there. "I need to sell a horse."

She clears her throat. There's a pause. "What horse?"

"Banks. Do you think he's worth ten thousand?"

"Uh, yeah you can probably get more for him." There's some rustling, and then her voice comes through the line crisper. "What's this about?"

"I just need him sold pretty quick. For at least ten thousand."

"Okay, I can start checking around tomorrow. But Nora are you okay? You're calling me about selling a horse at nearly midnight."

I grimace. Not very considerate of me is it? I hop up on the pickup bed and debate how much to say.

"Is this about your uncle?"

I swallow and it feels like a piece of glass. "Ian needs the money. He was going to sell his good horse." I sigh. There was a way around that, until...

I cut the thought off. I can't go back and put the calves in the lot.

"How does Banks get roped into this?"

Pulling one leg up on the metal bed, I launch into the whole story of the calves and how that has us where we are now. "He doesn't need to be worrying about money right now, and he wouldn't be if I'd closed the blooming gate."

A heavy sigh fills the phone line. "Nora."

I move to lean back against the headache rack, my throat tight.

"Nothing you can do for him is going to fix him." The words ooze out of her slowly, gently.

The air leaves my lungs even as I know she's right. I want it to, though. I want to do enough that he'll come back in the door and be the same Uncle Ian that met me in the cafe.

"It's not a debt you have to pay off. It's a fight only Ian can fight."

My heart beats in my ears. Nothing I can do... *Nothing*.

I pinch a pickin string on the headache rack between my fingers harder and harder trying to compensate for the ache in my chest. An ache of watching on as a handcuffed bystander. I want to be able to *do* something for him.

"It's alright, girl. We'll get 'em next week."

I keep causing messes in a world that he's already drowning in, and he waves it off.

Not a debt... I can't pay it off. A tear trickles its way down my cheek and then several more follow behind it. I let them fall.

"Your uncle is proud of you. You don't have to prove anything to him—or to any of us."

I wipe my nose on the cuff of my shirt sleeve.

"From everything I know about your uncle he just likes you around. To hear your voice and just visit. I'm sure those are his best days."

The floodgates open, and I suck in a shuddering breath. The ugliest cry from the very depths of my gut folds me up. Knees pulled up and head resting on them, I grip the phone like a lifeline.

My knuckles ache and eyes burn. "What do I do?" I croak the words out between gasps for oxygen.

"Just be there." Mindi's voice is soft. Almost too soft to hear.

A nod rubs my forehead against my knees. My hat falls to the flatbed with a soft thud. Being with a wisp of the strongest man I know is harder than anything else she could have told me.

"You let me tend to things here tomorrow. You just be there."

I wipe under my eyes. "Thank you." It comes out in a whimper. I put my hat back on my head and let my legs hang off the side of the truckbed.

I got so off track, Lord. I hope it's not too late to come back to the right one.

"Nor?" Another smooth voice, but not on the phone this time.

I close my eyes. *How many times does the poor man have to see me cry today?*

Hopping off the bed, I try to put at least a little pep in my step. "Yeah, I'm here."

The shadows his hat casts in the parking lamp glow hide his eyes. When I come around in front of the pickup his shoulders drop and he puts a hand on each of my shoulders. "Did you get your phone call made?" Each word comes out halted, measured.

I turn my phone over in my palms. "Yeah, I did."

"Good." His hands drop and he stuffs them in his pockets. "Do you want food? Denise and I tried to find some in the hospital but the cafeteria is already closed. There's a Whataburger down the road."

"Sure, sounds good." It really doesn't. Food sounds awful right now, but I need a minute before I go back in there.

Chapter 25

The pickup wheels stop rolling and the diesel's idle fills in the silence. Eight hours later and in the daylight, the hospital doesn't look any more inviting. I swallow and force my eyes to edge over enough to see James. How does the man exist in one continual state of okayness?

A glow of orange shines on the side of the big five story building from the morning sun. A plastic bag droops a little where condensation weighs it down. The cab smells like fast-food breakfast, but right now that smells pretty darn good.

My lower back aches and I shift in the seat. Hotel beds are always a gamble. "Are you sure you don't mind coming back to pick me up?"

James stretches and rests his hand on the back of my seat. A smug grin rests on his lips. "What would you do if I did?"

Heat flares up my cheeks. "Go home and come back in my own pickup, I guess."

"I don't mind. Academy isn't that far away. I think I can entertain myself by window shopping for guns."

"You can come inside too. I didn't mean to put you out of that either."

He shakes his head. "I'll stop in before we leave town."

I nod and lift the orange and white striped plastic bag. "I don't know how long I'll be."

"Take your time." His voice is smooth like a slicked off colt's back.

I almost feel like hugging him, but the console is in the way, and that'd just be awkward. "Thanks." It comes out a whisper.

After jamming my hat on my head, I push the pickup door open. I start the little trek for the rolling doors and sterilized air. No more sleep than I got last night, it's amazing I feel half as alive as I do. God's grace and a healthy dose of anticipation is about all I've got to thank for that.

An older couple waits on the curb, her hand tucked into the crook of his arm. I smile as I pass them. One day I hope my kids get to watch Ian and Denise love each other like that. I swallow a little wad of ache out of my throat.

Hope. I won't quit.

The lobby is quiet as I skirt around the chairs and to the elevators. One set of silver doors rolls back almost immediately. It takes a bit of coaxing for me to step on. Just because I need to have this conversation doesn't really mean I'm looking forward to it.

The contraption dings and I pull in a breath. I step out, strides are long and sure. Six of them, and I'm at the little microphone button. I press it.

"How can I help you?"

"I'm here to see Ian Kelly—room 312."

In just a few seconds the doors click and I mumble a "thank you" as I step away to push one open. My boot heels click on the floor. The sound echoes in my ears, but the ladies don't seem to notice.

Two quick light raps on the door of room 312. I close my eyes for a second. My heart pounds against my rib cage. In slow motion, I push the handle down and step inside. There's a curtain pulled, so it's a couple strides before I take in the drab cream colored walls.

Just then Denise pops out of the bathroom. A smile spreads across her face, but the first words I hear are Ian's.

"Hey girl."

I beg my face not to crumble as my eyes shift to him sitting up in the bed. "Hey," I croak out. The word triggers my brain back into function, and I hold up the sack. "I brought food." It's the second time I've brought Whataburger up here in the last ten hours.

"Yes." Denise gathers Ian's wallet and some papers off the rolling hospital table.

Denise pulls out the paper bags with our individual orders. Paper bags crinkle as she decides who's is what and then hands me Ian's unsweet tea. It's all he's allowed to have right now. I pass it to him, resting my other hand on the cool white plastic of his bed frame.

"Thank you." He sets it in his lap. "Come here."

My throat chokes on my own spit as I lean over to hug him, careful not to bump the IV in his arm. It's a tight one—almost like before. "I've missed you."

"I'm going to refill my coffee. Y'all want some?" Denise's sweet voice fills the air.

My insides relax in gratitude. *She picks up on more than she lets on.* "That'd be good."

"I'll be back in a bit."

I run my palms down the thighs of my jeans and look around the room. The chair in the corner doesn't look too hard to move. I pull it up next to the hospital bed.

"How was you kids' trip to San Saba?"

My cheeks flame without my permission. *Thank goodness I still have my hat on and he can't tell.* "It was there. Didn't stay very long."

The sheets rustle and the bed groans.

I unwrap my biscuit. Getting it halfway to my mouth, I stop. It's going to sit on a ball of dread if I eat it before talking. One glance up at Ian, and I know he knows it too. *Dadgum he's too good at this.*

I wet my lips. There's no good place to start this.

"I—uh, I'm sorry." I swallow away the stickiness coating my mouth. "I've been trying to do enough that you won't worry, so you can use all your strength to get better. In the process, I've managed to help you get here." Pick at a nail. "And completely neglect what really matters."

"That's an awful lot to be carrying around." Ian rasps the words out.

My shoulders droop. It's been a little more than I realized.

The bed creaks as he holds down a button it its remote control. Sitting straighter, he pins me with his intense gaze. "Girl, this landing here is strictly of my own doings."

I run one fingernail under another. *But if I had been there...*

"I tried to convince myself I felt half decent. I wanted to be horseback, so I did." He cocks one eyebrow higher than the other. "Turns out that was way over doing it."

I can make that make sense in my head. If I was him I'd have gone crazy a while ago. Puzzling that out doesn't make my brain shut up though.

I steal a glance at his face. A face I'd do anything to keep disappointment from. Studying my half-dirty fingernails again, I swallow. "I've not done a good job just visiting with you."

He grips the styrofoam cup and swallows several gulps of tea. "I've missed your recounts of the days."

"I know." I'm not sure he even heard those words, but it's okay.

The grin gone, his voice returns to its weighed down tone. "I shouldn't have let so much fall on your shoulders. Everything looked so good when we'd pull up I didn't think much about it."

I shake my head even before he quits talking. "You had plenty else to keep up with." I look down at my going-to-town boots. "I didn't want to slip up and have the conversations we usually have with someone else, so I got scared and tried to just not need help."

"Girl." The word hangs heavy in the air for a long moment. "Why can't you talk about things with other people like you do me?"

I shrug my shoulders. "Just don't feel right. I didn't have those before I started running around with you." A dry chuckle follows the words. "Sounds stupid now."

He shakes his head. "Not stupid. But there sure ain't no skin off my nose if you talk to people. Tickles me pink to watch you getting along so well."

I can see how it would. Somehow I missed that before, but now it makes sense.

"What about James? You seem pretty comfortable with him."

In a flash, my cheeks are on fire. Since when exactly does mention of him cause such nonsense? My mouth opens, but no words come out. Probably better—none of them are in any kind of order in my head.

He laughs a deep laugh that brings a hint of life to his hollow cheeks. Even if it is at my expense, it cocoons me like a hug. I wish I could bottle that laugh up and save it for later. His big paw of a hand rests on my shoulder. I look up to meet soft forgiving eyes. Somehow I manage to keep my eyes from darting away.

"I'm proud of you, girl. You've grown a lot since hiding behind a menu so you didn't have to talk to me."

I duck my head, just like that afternoon at the restaurant he's talking about. I'd be okay if he forgot about that day altogether. Leaning over, I wrap my arms around him again.

"Thank you," I whisper. *Thank you for everything.*

My now cold Whataburger biscuit is gone when the door eases open. Denise appears with a whole drink carrier of cups. Her smile holds enough sunshine to light up the whole room. "I found coffee and brought you more tea for back up."

Ian's hand rests on hers for a moment as he takes a plastic cup from her. "Thank you, dear."

She hands me a styrofoam cup of steaming coffee. "Guess who I got a call from."

"Probably some doctor wanting money," Ian mutters.

Denise turns toward Ian with narrowed eyes. "It's Sunday." She lifts her own steaming styrofoam cup to her lips. "Owen Hicks. He and Wellman are headed up here."

Mr. Wellman. I've been thinking about him. I look up from my coffee to Ian.

He pushes the black and white navajo woven blanket from Denise's bag back off his legs. "We better clean out some chairs then." He eases his legs off the side and stills a moment.

Denise sets her cup down and plants herself at his side. "And where are you headed?"

He reaches for her hand and her arm snakes around his back. "Just up." In one slow motion he rises to his feet, leaning against Denise a bit.

I study the top of my coffee feeling like I'm infringing on his privacy by watching.

Ian stands a moment before letting go of Denise and shuffling slow, sure steps to the bathroom.

I grip my paper coffee cup hard until one side of the lid pops off. *It's not supposed to be this way.*

I rustle around the room folding blankets from the spare chair and throwing away trash. When Ian reappears, my head is down and my hands are busy. I watch his slow, even steps out of the corner of my eye. He makes it to the window and stares out.

Swallowing down a lump in my throat, I lean against the wall in the corner. I didn't even know it until now, but maybe this dark cloud is why I haven't made it up here much. It's hard to sit here and not be able to do a darn thing for him.

Ian's voice draws me out of my trance. "Have you met Owen?"

At his voice, I stand up straight. "No, sir, I haven't."

"He's a good kid. A little more city than what fits Kay and Wellman, but he's got a good head."

A knock sounds at the door. A nurse buzzes in and changes out the bag on top of the pole that follows Ian around. Before she leaves, there's another knock, and two men walk through the door.

The little half-bent shuffling man in the front scans the room. His smile blooms when he sees Denise, it grows just a hair more as his gaze passes over me, and then it flickers when his eyes land on Ian.

I know.

A part of me feels like apologizing, but I simply stand there. Mr. Wellman shuffles to Ian. The two men shake hands, and then Mr. Wellman wraps his left arm around Ian in a hug.

"I'm Owen Hicks. You must be Nora."

I look up. The younger Hicks towers above me. I shake his extended hand. "Yes sir. Nice to meet you."

"You too." He stands beside me, facing the rest of the room.

My eyes focus in as Mr. Wellman wraps Denise in a hug. There's gentleness in the older man's eyes and it seems to put a little strength in Denise's shoulders.

I swallow. *So many good people here.* And all of them have been through worse than they've had coming to them.

My phone vibrates in my pocket, and I pull it out. James has spent all the time he can burn at Academy.

You can come up here. Mr. Wellman and his son Owen are here.

I slide the device in my pocket. It vibrates again, but Mr. Wellman's shuffling my way.

"Miss Nora, how's life been treating you?"

I return the little man's hug. "It hasn't given me much time to get in trouble. How have you been?"

"Another day, another try."

"You're here. That's something." I smile. It's small, but one that spreads through my chest and down my arms. "Are you still on your place? I keep meaning to call you..." I don't voice the sorry excuse of being busy.

"I'm still there." He reaches for the back of a chair, hand shaking like the vibration of a motor. "We've put some cows back out there, and my grandson's been helping keep them straight."

Those words are music to my ears. I glance at Owen leaned up against the wall next to Ian's chair, visiting.

Mr. Wellman props his hat farther back on his head. "I hear you've been keeping the fort running."

"Trying to anyway." I tuck the tips of my fingers in my front pockets. *It hasn't fallen down completely yet.*

"You're doing more good than you know." He shifts around on his feet to gaze at Ian propped up in the chair. "He talks about you as much as he used to about Kayla."

Those darn tears claw a little farther up my throat. I press my lips together and wrap and arm around the aging man. "Thank you," I whisper.

Owen strides out of the room with his phone to his ear.

Wellman gestures to the chair Ian is propped up in. "I'm going to catch up with an old friend." He pats my shoulder and shuffles over to perch on the side of the thin hospital bed.

The pale wooden door eases open and James strides in, instantly locking eyes with me. He stands next to close enough I can feel his body heat, and I feel just a little bit stronger.

"Find anything you can't live without?" I whisper over my shoulder to him.

"A little ammo is all."

I don't have a chance to answer before Ian beckons James over. Handshakes, grins, and a few good laughs pass between the three generations of cowboys. Except for the steady ticking of Ian's IV machine, one could almost forget we're in a hospital.

Chapter 26

The orange sunset has faded into a dusky gray sky. The screech of James's trailer jack rolling down overpowers any birds chirping their goodnights.

I fell asleep three times on the drive back from the hospital, and I could again while standing up here against the pickup.

"We're good to go." James slaps the flatbed.

I wrangle myself back into his passenger seat. "Thank you for driving me around all over the country the last couple days."

He shifts the pickup in drive. "Of course. I'm glad I was with you."

My eyes cloud over with tears. "Me too."

"Do you still want to come over here and gather those calves up in the morning?"

Right. Tomorrow is Monday. I stare out the window as we pass a yellow van. *Should* we? Probably. Is getting up to beat the bushes *really* what I want to do in the morning? No, not really. "Umm, I guess I better ask Ian what he wants us to do."

Pushing my hat back a little, I run my hand down my face. "I guess you probably have stuff you need to catch up on since I kept you gone all weekend?"

"Nothing I can't put off an afternoon or two."

The pickup rolls to a stop at the stop sign on the edge of town. "Can I let you know in the morning? We don't have to start at daylight either way."

James flips on his blinker and swings the pickup and trailer in a wide right turn. "Yes ma'am."

"Thanks," I murmur.

Studying the outlines of bushes and fence posts, my eyes flutter shut. Too soon, a rattle jars me awake. One look around the pickup cab reminds me that all I left the house with yesterday morning was my wallet and phone in my pockets and a water jug.

"Thanks again for driving me." I push the pickup door open and slide into the powdery dirt.

James pushes his door open and meets me in front of the pickup. He holds out an arm and I lean into him. "Get some rest tonight."

"You too." I wabble my way across the caliche to the porch.

The porch creaks and the door sticks, but one good shove and I'm inside. I hang my hat on a peg and stumble to my room as the diesel's purr fades away. The weekend's adrenaline is all the way gone as I slip on shorts and a t-shirt and flop down on the bed.

I spend a few seconds staring at the ceiling, then I reach for my phone to shoot Denise a text.

I didn't want to wake Ian up. Whenever you get the chance will you ask him if he wants me to get the calves up to take to the sale tomorrow?

Rolling over on the bed, I close my eyes and breathe in the cool of the sheets.

The next thing I know, it's daylight outside, and my phone is ringing right by my ear. After blinking a couple of times, I can finally read Denise's name across the top of the screen.

"Hello," I mumble.

"Good morning, Nora. Did I wake you up?" The cheer in her voice breathes life into my veins.

I lick my lips and swallow before trying to talk again. "It's okay. How are you?"

"You'll never guess who came by to see Ian."

I rub my eyes with a knuckle and put feet on the bedside rug. *You're right. I'm not awake enough to guess my middle name right now.* "Who's that?"

"Clay, your boss."

I halt my shuffle in the bedroom doorway. *He finally went to see him.* "Oh really, what's he up to?"

Her voice drops a couple levels. "Clay brought Ian a check."

I grasp the door frame as my knees weaken. Several words start to form but never get out. *A check? And Ian took it?*

"Nora, it's exactly what we've been praying for."

The warmth of tears wells up behind my eyes. I don't try to stop my vision from blurring. One tear slides down my cheek and then another. *Exactly what they've been praying for.*

"That's great," I croak out.

"Oh! Ian's off the phone now. Here, talk to him."

I down a half glass of water I abandoned last night.

"Hey girl." His voice is a little hoarse and still weighed down with weakness, but it's cheery. "I told Clay not to go too hard on you. I've been keeping you busy."

"What'd he have to say to that?" The words come out with a crippled laugh.

A few beeps and mumbled words fill the line. Then it's Ian's words that are a little crippled. "He said he's sure you did just fine."

I sniff back the tears that threaten to slide down my cheeks. "You gotta quit being sappy on me, you're making me cry." I reach for the coffee grounds and measure them into a fresh filter.

A couple moments pass. "Girl," his voice is thick, "It's just cause I know you're tough enough to."

You have to be tough enough to cry. I can hear the words in the exact tender voice he told them to me last year on my porch.

He clears his throat and returns with a more chipper tone. "Well anyway, Denise told me you texted. Don't worry about the calves, we'll get them another week."

I press start on the coffee maker and lean back against the counter. "Sounds good. They ought to be good and healthy."

"Maybe I'll be horseback with you and that old coworker of yours when we do."

My cheeks combust into fire red flares. The smirk in his voice implies everything his words don't. "If you're mounted we might not even need James."

Ian's laugh is fuller than I've heard in a long while. "Maybe you ought to keep him around anyway."

Chapter 27

Is it okay if I pick you up about thirty minutes early? I need to pick a few things up on the way to the party.

James's text brings me back from my own little world of patching fence. *It's already Saturday?* I better get rolling if I'm going to be ready for his buddy's party.

Sounds good.

I tie the last little piece off and throw the tools in the pickup. The engine rattles to life, and the clock pops up on the radio. *2:13.*

Good grief! I'm about to be late.

I job the pickup into gear and turn it for the house. He'll be here in under an hour. At this rate, I'll be leaving it up to deodorant and a fresh shirt to make me presentable.

I try to envision what's in the back corner of my closet. It doesn't get used enough for me to picture many options. There's a sweater, but September highs in the 90s aren't sweater weather.

The front tire hits a hole in the road, jostling me against the door and almost into the middle seat. Maybe I should just worry about the clothes once they're in front of me. For a Saturday, the roads are busy, and none of the drivers want to go eighty-five with me. It takes the full twenty minutes to get to the turn off and onto the home stretch.

At the house, I hang my hat on a kitchen chair. Then I scour the closet. I almost grab a faithful pink button down, but instead I opt for a light blue shirt with lace sleeves. The party is just a couple hours long; I can manage being half fancy for that long.

As I'm tucking the bottom into my jeans, my phone rings. 'Ian' reads at the top of the screen. I slide the green circle across, stab at the speaker button, and put the phone on the bathroom counter. "Hello?"

"Hey girl, what are you up to?"

I buckle my belt and look in the mirror. Getting halfway there to being a human. "Ah, I'm getting ready to go to a party." *Since when do I go to parties?*

"A party? What kind of party?" His tone is teasing.

I pull a pair of boot earrings from my horseshoe nail box. "A surprise birthday party for a buddy of James's. He's turning thirty."

A humored laugh I haven't heard from him in a while floats through the phone. "With James, huh?"

My cheeks color. Like I put lipstick on them instead of my lips. "Yes."

"Ask her if she'll come over for dinner." Denise's voice is distant, but still comes through clearly.

"Did you hear that?"

"Yes sir, but I'm going to have to take a rain check." Earrings in, I put that box up and pull out the little plastic container of bobby pins.

"Trading us in."

"Hey now," I say with a pin in my mouth. I pull it out and scoop a lock of hair to pin back. "Rain check, I said. How about tomorrow after church?"

Ian laughs. "That'll be just fine."

A diesel engine rattles outside. Sliding the other bobby pin in my hair, I look in the mirror. Mascara highlighting my eyelashes, hair pinned back, and a shirt that shows I have some kind of figure besides a stick holding plaid material up, I almost look girly. The engine's rattle dies outside.

"I'm going to let you go. James just pulled up."

"Alright. Y'all stay out of trouble."

A girlish giggle bubbles out of me. "We'll try."

His chuckle vibrates through the phone. "Y'all have fun. Talk to you later."

"Talk to you later." Just as I slide my phone in my jeans pocket, there's James's knock. I glance one more time in the mirror before leaving the bathroom.

Hopefully my boot heels on the hard floor carries onto the porch so James doesn't think I'm just leaving him hanging. I can't bring myself to yell for him to come in though. I reach for the door handle as butterflies flare in my stomach. Hopefully my cheeks aren't still flaming red.

"Well darn, Nor, I nearly don't recognize you."

My cheeks are definitely red now if they weren't already.

I step back so I'm not blocking the doorway. Am I supposed to give him a hug? I'm *not* shaking his hand.

James stuffs his hands in his jeans pockets. I guess he doesn't know either. At least we're on the same page.

I jerk a thumb over my shoulder before spinning on my heels to my bedroom. "I, uh, just need to grab a jacket." When the sun goes down it might accidentally cool off enough I need a little extra.

"Alright. No hurry."

Six half decent jackets stare at me from the back of my closet. I have no idea what goes with this shirt. I reach for a crisp tan canvas jacket, but at the last second pull a lined denim one off the hanger. Denim goes with everything.

"You think you're going to need that?" He holds the door open for me and we step out on the porch.

I give him a side eye glance. "I get cold in the evenings, okay?" I hang back enough that he has to step off the porch first.

"Whatever makes you happy." He chuckles as he leads the way around to the front and opens the passenger door of his pickup.

"Thank you," I murmur and squeeze on the edge of the seat as if it's not big enough for two of me.

Goodnight. I wasn't this jittery when we went to San Saba.

After he's settled in the driver's seat, I catch him looking at me out of the corner of my eye. I wind my fingers together.

Words. Surely this would be less awkward if there were words being tossed around.

"How's Ian?"

I swallow. I'm not one for small talk either. "He's home. I talked to him earlier; he's in good spirits." The smile on my face betrays the ache that the weakness in his voice put in my gut.

James's gaze lingers on me for a long moment. The grinding of tires on the rubble strips forces his eyes back on the road. "I'll swing by after church tomorrow if he's up for it."

"I'm eating lunch with them tomorrow. You should come." The words are out of my mouth before I even know what they are.

Panicked thoughts bombard me. What if Ian isn't up for more visitors? What if Denise doesn't want to feed another mouth? I should have asked them first. Who am I, anyway? Inviting people to eat.

I chew on the inside of my lip. It'll all be fine. Denise would have told him to come anyway.

"Nor?"

My head snaps around. "Sorry, what did you say?"

He punches it to get across the road before a car gets closer. "I'm getting drinks to take to the party. What do you want?"

I watch a sports car zip from the gas pump. "I'm okay."

He parks in front of the convenience store and rests his elbow on the console. "I'm glad you're okay, but that's not what I asked."

A little giggle escapes my lips. I still don't have an actual answer to his question. I glance up to meet his steady stare.

After a few dragged out seconds he shakes his head. "What do you not want?"

"To not make decisions?" Another giggle—where are these coming from?

Chuckling, he opens the door. "I'll be back."

Chapter 28

Ian's pens are quiet when my headlights shine over them. There are a couple horses in the corner pen by the water trough. I cut the engine and button my jean jacket up against the cool that has moved in overnight. If it keeps this up we'll be wearing sweatshirts for the first of November.

Slipping out of the cab, I reach behind the seat for Banks's bridle. I picked him at the last minute this morning. I don't want to feel the weather change under my saddle while busting these soggy calves out of the bushes.

"You're catching me late." Ian meets me outside the saddle house.

The last three weeks since getting out of the hospital sure have done wonders for Ian. His voice holds strength I haven't heard in months. It's back to the one I can pick out just about everywhere.

I turn and wrap my arms around his jacket-covered torso in a tight hug. "I think I'm early."

He returns my hug, letting go with a grin half-covered by his mustache. *Darn, it's good to see him feeling this good again.*

"Maybe so." He heads for the building, the jingle of his spurs marking his steps.

I rummage around under my pile of bridles, managing to pull my leggins out without bringing the entire collection with them. They're cool as I slide into them. I'm sure not adjusted to mornings in the fifties yet.

The rattle of a trailer over the caliche road turns my head as I close the gates to my own trailer. I squint into the headlights. James's face comes more into view through the fuzz of the lights the closer he pulls up.

When the engine stops running and after the slam of a door, I call a "Morning" over Banks's back.

"Good morning. I guess I need to adjust my clock. I thought I was going to be early." James's spurs jingle and rocks rustle under his feet.

I laugh and toss the halter in my pickup bed. "You're not late."

The trailer latch screeches, clomping hooves sound on the wooden floor, and then the closing screech. More hoof beats, but this time they're softer.

James's voice is smooth and closer when he says, "How are you this morning?"

I turn and my face is mere inches from James's chest. *Goodness! How'd he get so close?* "I'm good. How are you?"

"Just fine. Ready to pen us some cattle."

I'm focused on a knot in Banks's mane, but I can hear the smile in his voice. It brings the curve back to my face too. The squeak of a gate latch draws my gaze to the pens as Ian leads Sailor out of the alley.

Savoring the hint of greasewood on the air, I pull in a slow breath and close my eyes. *Thank you, Lord.* Two dang special men and a cool pony—I couldn't ask for more.

Ian and James exchange "good mornings" and shake hands. Then they both look at me.

"Where do you want to start?" Ian asks, eyes trained on me.

Why exactly am I supposed to have the plan? "I guess we ought to drive to the back side first."

Ian's mustache parts in a grin and he throws an arm around my shoulders. "You driving?"

"No sir." *What part of me not being in charge did he miss?*

Ian and James's laughter melts together. The jingle of spurs and clipping of horse hooves mixes with the laughter in perfect tune.

Ian leads the way past the end of my pickup and trailer to his that sits a little closer to the house. "Denise is going to drive us around there, so we don't have to go back for the pickup after we get these cattle penned."

Thank goodness someone has a plan.

Reins looped around the saddle horns, we load our horses in the trailer. James jumps up on the old flatbed and then offers me a hand up. Ian gets in the cab, rolls the window down, and hangs his arm down the side of the door.

Denise speed walks from the house, waving.

"Good morning!" I call in unison with James.

"Morning! I'll try not to buck y'all off back there."

James laughs and leans against the headache rack. "We'll hold on tight."

The wheels start rolling. I re-situate my hat so the front band rests on my eyebrows. My brains might suction out, but my hat won't fly off. The wind starts blowing my stray hairs all around my face. It's cool air, and I nestle into my jacket a little more.

I want a movie of this morning that I can play over and over again—to savor.

Denise stops the rig in the middle of the road almost at the back of the pasture. As the passenger door opens, Ian steps out, and James and I scramble off the bed of the pickup.

James swings the trailer gates open. His horse is the first to back out. The gelding shies as James reaches for the reins but then stands quietly beside him. Banks backs out one slow, sure step at a time. I take the reins off the saddle horn and lead him out of the way.

I tighten my cinch as the trailer gates bang shut. Turning Banks in a little circle, I tug my leggins up a notch before getting on.

It's a minute or two before Ian gets mounted. Once he's on, he sits tall and lifts his rope to sit over his leg. "We'll make a sweep on the west side and throw them on the right a'way. Then we'll see what we have and maybe go on the east side."

"Sounds good." Lately it's seemed the cattle have been staying on the west side, if they didn't decide to move on us last night.

"James, will you take the outside? Just arc around until you hit the corner in a quarter mile or so."

James nods. "Yes sir."

Ian's gaze swivels my direction. "You go in the middle?"

"Yes sir."

James straightens out his reins. "See y'all around," he says with a grin. He turns his horse north and strikes a trot.

I feel Ian's gaze on me, but I don't look over. The knick on my saddle horn is all of a sudden quite fascinating.

Ian chuckles. "It might be better if you had red hair—at least he'd be looking for the same color as the Hereford's."

I hold up a hand to hide behind as my neck flushes hot.

He laughs, full and loud. Sailor's ear flicks back. Ian scoots him up next to me and puts a hand on my shoulder. "Let's go find some cattle."

Yes, please.

I turn Banks to the right and tap his sides for a trot. "Have fun," I holler over my shoulder. *My cheeks are probably still red.*

Banks's rocking little trot carries us for several minutes. No tracks and no cattle. Then his ears stand on end, and his steps become high. I pull him up and concentrate on listening. Distant brush cracks and then a sharp "hey!" that trails off into other words I can't understand.

The crackling gets closer. I circle back to the north a hair. Through the web of brush I catch sight of red hide with a couple white faces sprinkled in. They're headed to the middle alright. Quick, fast, and in a hurry. Ian's not going to be doing much stopping them.

Banks is already on high alert, so all I have to do is relax into the saddle and push the reins forward for him to be off. It's a rough trot as he picks his way out of the thicket.

"Just a second, bud," I murmur. As sure as I get too far ahead of them, they'll come out behind me.

It really is only seconds before brush pops just ahead of us on the edge of the thicket. A high headed momma cow billows out with a big calf at her side, and the rest of the herd on her heels. Banks stretches his trot out to long quick strides and angles toward the cow.

"Hey momma," I growl out the words as my head snaps back around to make sure her followers don't squirt out behind me. They're still following her trail, so I squeeze my legs against Banks's sides. He jumps a bush, lopes a few strides, and jumps another.

We're even with the lead cow. Pressing into her, I glance back just in time to see a wild look come into the calf's eyes. I grimace and swing my left leg out to connect with Banks just behind his shoulder. Though I barely touch him, he's already turning back. His chest lands right in front of the calf. The thick calf whirls back the other way, but his momma's side isn't where it was. She's grabbed another gear.

The calf throws in with the rest of them, but before Banks can gather himself up to head her off again, James and his blue roan streak by.

"Hey stupid!" He hollers, hand coming down to slap at his leggins.

I don't get to see what the cow's doing to earn the tongue lashing that she receives. Her followers have snapped out of their blind trotting and each start their own trail due south.

Making a sweep between them and the thicket, I catch sight of the roan's fancy footwork. James circles the cow tight to the right and jumps over to turn the calf back before stopping.

The other eight pairs have turned into each other, so I rein Banks around in a small circle to back off the herd. He tingles with just as much adrenaline that dances in my veins. I put a hand on his neck to steady us both.

The roan is coated in sweat, and his nostrils flare with each breath. James straightens out a rein and then looks across the herd at me. "I'm sure glad you showed up." He pants almost as bad as his horse does.

I swing my gaze from one side of the herd to the other. "Where'd you find them?"

He points back to the northwest. "Just out of that corner. They took off, and this is the first time they've slowed down." The lead cow takes a few steps away from the herd. James prods his roan for a few steps. "Don't you even think about it."

A cow on my side picks up her head and takes a step toward the brush. I lift the reins, and Banks takes a step toward her.

"How far do you think—" The lead cow starts off at a trot. James and the roan jump to get ahead of her. His voice rises to carry over his shoulder. "The right a'way is?"

The rest of the cows start off a little slower. I push a calf up to go with them and then kick out to the side. "Ah, probably—"

Before I finish, Sailor's big bay chest barrels through the mesquite right in front of the lead cow. The cow whirls back, splitting the herd as she cuts through them.

Several scatter to the south, and I turn Banks after them. "Come on girls!"

Banks gets right up close to them, bending them back into the middle. When I pull up, James is a couple horse lengths away, and Ian's on the other side. The cattle mill in the middle. We sit for a minute.

"Nora."

My head snaps up and my eyes look across at Ian.

"You lead them across to the right a'way." I guess he sees the wheels turning in my head, because he points. "Just diagonal across toward that old windmill tower."

I nod and point Banks out in front of the herd. We start out at a steady walk to put a little distance between us and the cattle.

Before I skirt around a patch of mesquites, I look back over my shoulder. The cattle are balled up in a tight circle. A few more strides, and I look back to see the lead cow trotting, aimed for the space between Ian and I. Easing Banks over in front of her path, I keep an eye trained over my shoulder.

Fifteen minutes into the trail to the water lot and they've only tried to scatter twice. The lead cow is right on Banks's tail and tries to push by every few minutes, but the rest of them have settled into a plodding line.

Shifting in the saddle, I turn to watch behind me. James's roan jumps a bush angled back toward the fence. Hopefully whatever else he runs across back there handles a little better than these girls.

Chapter 29

The Ford's engine purrs behind me, but I can barely hear it, much less Ian, over the nineteen bawling calves in the trailer. Ian hands me his credit card and a paper with their mailing address on it.

Out of the corner of my eye, I watch Denise approach James with a bag.

"I think there's enough diesel in it to get you there." Ian manages to say between uproars of bawling.

"We'll make it."

He rests his big paw of a hand on my shoulder. "Thank y'all for taking them."

James strolls up to us, a plastic bag in hand. "You driving?"

I shake my head. "No sir, that is all you."

"Alright." He holds out the plastic bag. "You get to hand me food then."

"I can do that."

Ian waves and starts toward Denise. "Stay out of trouble," he calls over his shoulder.

A girlish little grin spreads across my face. It doesn't wipe away. Thankfully James is already on his way around the front of the pickup and doesn't see it.

Once we're on the pavement, I unwrap the sandwiches Denise sent with us and hand one to James. I open the big bag of chips and set them up on top of the cup holders. Lunch is served.

The crunching of food with soft country music in the background fills the first hour of the drive. After we're done eating, I fold the chip bag down and put the sandwich paper in the grocery sack. A few minutes pass. I glance out of the corner of my eye at James. He's got a wrist cocked over the top of the steering wheel.

Licking my lips, I muster up words. "Can I tell you something?" It comes out so soft I'm not sure James could hear them over the purr of the engine, but his head turns my way.

"Go for it."

I sit up a little taller in the seat and weave my fingers together. "I've been thinking a lot lately about what you said on the way to San Saba."

"Nor—"

I shake my head. "Please, let me say this." *I have to say this. It's been eating at me too long now.*

"Alright." He leans against the console, watching the road and then sparing a glance my way.

"You were right. I enjoyed your company, but then it felt like I enjoyed it *too* much. I was out here smiling, and Ian was fighting for his life." I swallow. *The hard part's out. Now just to say this without crying.* "Ian's the only reason that I'm here. He was the first person I could really talk to. If it hadn't been for that when Wade sold off the heifers—it would have been a lot worse."

James's Adam's apple bobs.

I untangle my fingers and pick at a nail. "I think the reason I kept ignoring your calls and stuff was because I was worried I'd get too used to it and talk to you more than Ian."

I stare out the window as my throat tightens up, heart beating about twice as fast as it should. *What if James thinks it's as stupid as it sounds?*

"I—I never want to replace him." A nervous, airy chuckle leaves this brick of a man. "I can't even come close to touching that man."

Slowly swiveling my head back around, my shoulders lose their tension as I take in the patience on James's face. *I don't know anyone that can.*

"I'm sorry, Nor." His jaw moves a couple times without sound coming out. When words do come they are low and a little raspy. "I just wanted to help you. I can't make Ian better, but I can make sure you're not fixing pipelines by yourself. Anything to make sure you know you aren't alone."

Looking out the window, I wipe under my eyes. Inside my chest, my heart puffs up like Dune's winter coat—fluffy and asking for a hug. The pickup slows. My vision is a little blurry as I look over at James, my eyebrows knitted together.

He pulls over on the side of the road and puts Ian's pickup in park. Turning to me, his eyes are soft yet intense. As much as I want to, I can't look away. He reaches across the console and brushes back a little hair that stuck to my cheek.

"No matter what happens." A little quirky smile pulls at his lips ever so slightly. "If you and Ian take off for Arizona to work cattle, or you stay in that little corner of highway 67, I'm just a phone call away."

I press my lips into a smile and squeak out, "Thank you."

"I know this is hard for you, but I can't imagine *how hard* it is for you." He lifts my hat and stares into my eyes. "Hit me next time I'm not getting that."

I snort a laugh. "We can work on it together." The word 'together' leaves my mouth and my face turns stop sign red. *Man I like the sound of that.*

He puts his hands on the steering wheel, then takes them off again. "This isn't where or how I really wanted to do this, but I can't keep beating around the bush." He takes in a big breath and looks over at me again. "Can we make this whole 'I'm here for you' thing official? Nora, will you be my girlfriend?"

That stop sign red rises back to my cheeks. If James keeps doing this I'll look like a tomato forever.

Girlfriend. So official. I lift my eyes and look into James's own red face. My stomach flutters with butterflies. "Yes, I'd like that."

James's smile spreads across his face like a grass fire with a high wind behind it. He puts his hand up on the console like last time we were in the pickup together. I slide my fingers between his and melt into the seat.

I never realized how good being James Butler's girlfriend sounded.

Chapter 30

Ian's back door swings open at James's hand with only the tiniest little creak. Not like the one at my house. I step in first and hang my hat on a peg. Sweet cornbread smells fills the air. My stomach growls. It hasn't even been that long since the sandwich Denise packed for us.

"There they are." Denise turns, pan in her hands. "Just in time."

"Smells good." I pull Ian's credit card out of my back pocket. "Where should I put this before I forget?"

"You can put it on his desk in there." Denise nods over her shoulder.

Ian is leaned back napping in his recliner when I walk by. I make my steps light. Leaving the card on top of a closed leather book, I turn back to ease by his chair again.

"Tires make it alright?"

Stopping in my tracks, I back petal a couple steps. *Playing possum.* "They did." I lean against the big leather chair next to his.

"Good." He leans forward and the back of the recliner snaps to attention. "What do you think?"

I perch on the arm of the chair. "I think it's been the best day in a while." *In so many ways.*

The foot rest of his recliner snaps down into the chair. "Me too."

I glance toward the kitchen and knit my fingers together. "So James—" My knee bounces and I lick my lips before finishing. "Asked me to be his girlfriend."

Ian's eyebrows reach for his hairline. "And?"

A new wave of heat shoots up my neck. "You don't actually need me to tell you that. You already know."

A deep laugh vibrates out of his chest. "You think so, do you?"

"I know so."

His big hand plops on top of my knee, forcing it to stop bouncing. "You mean I've got to share your spare time now?"

I pick at a callous on my palm and force the edges of my lips to perk up. "Something like that." He's joking, but dang that fear still haunts me. What if I can't juggle two really important relationships?

The chair pops as he pushes out of it. I almost launch in to help him, but he is steady as a rock on his feet. He's stronger than he was in the hospital six weeks ago even if his movements are a touch measured still.

The hand he rests on my shoulder is gentle and not at all for stability. "I'm happy for you, girl."

"Thank you," I say into his chest, wrapping my arms around him for a hug.

"Supper is ready!" Denise calls, followed by a clattering of dishes.

Her timing couldn't be better. For a moment I wonder if she and James could hear, but even if they did it's just one less conversation I have to have.

Ian squeezes me in the hug before letting go. He doesn't say anything, but his eyes glitter a little.

I wonder if Kayla ever came home and had this conversation with him. What would his reaction have been if it was her? I'll never know, but that's okay.

IN BETWEEN PASTURES

Passing Ian's seat at the corner of the table, I slide into the one opposite him. James beelines it to the chair beside me. I smile at him. *Man, I've been doing that a lot lately.*

Denise slides a bottle of salad dressing on the table and then takes a seat next to Ian. She looks over at him, and he bows his head. I follow suit, closing my eyes. James's hand touches mine under the table, our fingers intertwining. Thank goodness everyone's head is bowed, because heat flares up my cheeks.

Thank you Lord for today. It's been about as close to perfect as it could be.

Ian's prayer is short, and then the dishes start being passed around. Denise serves steaming chili out of a big pot. Corn bread, lettuce, and salad fixings spin around the table from one pair of hands to another.

"Ranch?" James cocks the bottle in my direction.

I split my cornbread with my fork. "No thanks."

"You eat that rabbit food dry?" His eyebrows sit wonky on his forehead as his gaze swivels around to me.

I shrug my shoulders. "It still goes down."

A couple minutes of utensils against plates and bowls pass as chili is scarfed up. The quiet is so peaceful, a moment untainted.

"Nora, when do I get to watch these kiddos you've been coaching?" Ian's voice mixes with the clinks as if it was made to.

I set down my spoonful of chili. My eyes dart to each person at the table as if they're the ones that have been coaching kids. James is the only other one that has had a spare moment to, and I'm pretty sure he hasn't even watched. "I think the last playday is in two weeks."

Maybe? I don't know how many I've missed.

"Are you going to ride with them?"

James's elbow bumps mine. "Yeah, you should."

I narrow my eyes at him. *Don't encourage it.* "No, no. I'm just a cheerleader by the time it's a playday."

Ian's eyes flick between James and I and grins across the table. *Gosh, these two are going to be a handful together.*

"It'll be on a Saturday?"

I nod, chewing on a piece of rabbit food.

"We ought be to be back from town." He looks to Denise and she nods.

Her hand reaches out and rubs his arm tenderly.

I want a love like that. Stronger than ever after two trials no one should have to face. I glance at James out of the corner of my eye. I think it may have found me.

My smile is thin. Treatment. Cancer. They're still words we have to deal with. As much as I wish today wiped them all away, it didn't. But we'll make it. All of us together will make it through all the highs and lows until Ian is free and clear.

***

The thud of Banks's hooves on the trailer floor dies away as he gets to the front. I pull the gate around and slip the pin into place. Lingering at the end of the rig, I pick at a long finger nail. James is loading his roan in his trailer. The ring of James's spurs gets louder and then stops.

I stare at his worn boots and fight back the idiotic smile on my face. I look up into his blue eyes.

"Well, you got a busy day tomorrow?" The sunset glow bounces off of his straw hat, giving it an orange hue.

I shake my head. "Not too bad. You?"

He leans up against the trailer gate and slips an arm around my back. I lean into him. "Do you want to help me move some cows?"

"What time?" As naturally as possible, I unfold my arm from in front of me and hover it behind his back. Just close enough that it touches him but without clinging to him like a lifeline.

"Whatever time you want, preferably in the daylight."

I roll my eyes at him. *A lot of help that you are, sir.* "Let me get to the backside in the morning and see what's fallen apart back there then I might can."

"They're your cows."

My eyebrows knit together. *I don't have cows.*

"The trailer load from the last set of heifers you calved for Wade."

I jerk back away from him, bouncing on my toes. "Is Ninety-four out there?"

He grins and reaches for my arm, pulling me back to him. "Maybe, I don't really know."

"I'll see if I can make it over." My voice is a higher pitch than usual. It almost squeaks.

"You coming to see me or the cows?"

Sheepishly, I lift one shoulder. "Both, maybe."

He pulls me even closer to him, pushing the hat off my head. It fumbles in his hand a couple times before he has a good hold of it. I lay my head against his chest, for once not crying while I do.

"You better get on the road before it gets dark." He lets me go and hands me my hat back. "Tell me when you get home?"

I shove my hat into place. "Yes. Drive safe."

"You too." Lifting his hat, he leans close to me. His breath is warm against my face. A moment's hesitation, and then his lips touch ever so gently on my cheek. "Goodnight, sweetheart."

Breathlessly, I whisper, "Goodnight."

Spur rowels jingling, I breathe in the evening air before getting in my pickup. The trailer rattling behind the pickup tires is music to my ears.

I stop where the dirt road meets the Farm to Market one. My pickup mirrors are filled with orange and pink melted together in a sunset. I pull out my phone and take a picture of it.

"They say pictures are worth a thousand words," I whisper.

I'll frame this one—to always say everything I can't about today.

Glossary

Leggins

Leather pants, minus the seat, that protect the cowboy(girl)'s legs from brush and weather elements.

Pickin' string

A short piece of rope, usually carried on one's saddle and leggins. It is a universal tool, being used to tie gates close, to tie down a wayward calf, or as a dog leash.

Cake

Feed high in protein and shaped into cubes for cattle.

Hackamore

Headgear to ride a horse in that does not have a bit. Instead, it has a noseband called a **Bosal**.

Honda

Located on one end of the rope a honda is what the rope passes through on its way to making a loop.

Acknowledgements

In Between Pastures has had many cheerleaders and coaches and fans!

Thank you to everyone who shared excitement for book two.

Forever a thank you to my own personal Uncle Ian, Brazos Davis, you're forever missed. You pulled me out from underneath my rock and challenged me to do hard things. Uncle Ian and Nora have been born from that and will carry on your torch into the world.

Thank you to my brainstorm buddy, editing wizard, and first fan (literally) Amanda Willings! Thank you for loving from the very start and all the many times you've read over the outline and SO many drafts! You're such a blessing as a friend and helper.

Juliet and Alabama, you've both been along for all the versions of Nora's story! Thank you for sticking with us on this journey and pushing me to dive deeper, especially when it's uncomfortable.

Jen Lindsey, thank you for your edits on *In Between Pastures*! You gave such helpful insights into Nora's character and threads of the story I couldn't pick up for myself. Very grateful for you work!

Annie, thank you for doing such a thorough job on line edits!

Allie, Laura, Amanda, Juliet, Faith—Thank y'all for being such awesome Beta readers and fans of Nora and her world!

To all the fans, thank you for loving Nora and sharing how her world encourages you!

Author's note

Unfortunately cancer is no longer a rarity in our world.

Dear reader, if you or a loved one has walked that road I am deeply sorry and pray for God's hand of comfort and healing over you.

This journey doesn't look the same for anyone. It's diagnosed at different times, has different (but no less horrific) symptoms, and there's a variety of treatment options.

I don't write on this topic lightly. My own personal Uncle Ian, my Uncle Brazos, walked the road of cancer beginning in 2020. Much like Nora, I watched from the ranch, wanting to keep the stress of the animals off his plate.

I have done my best to handle this topic with the care and delicacy that it deserves. Ian's road may not look like your loved one's. I modeled it off the one I got to witness and admit that my family usually takes a less traveled route. Treating cancer was no different.

I hope that no matter the treatment pattern you see Ian take that the heart of a fighter sticks with you. Keep grabbing and clawing at life with God as your refuge and your community's support!

Free Gift

Have you ever found yourself close to someone walking through a hard season and at a loss for how to pray for them?

Get a 7 Day Prayer Guide for Sharing One Another's Burdens in your inbox today!

Like Nora here in *In Between Pastures* we want to do something when our loved ones are suffering and prayer is the best thing we can do! This guide gives you seven days of prompts of what to pray for, scripture to back it up, and a written prayer example.

Go to sequoyahbranham.com/afteribp[1] to get yours today!

---

1. http://sequoyahbranham.com/afteribp

Did you love *In Between Pastures*? Then you should read *In The Company Of Cows*[2] by Sequoyah Branham!

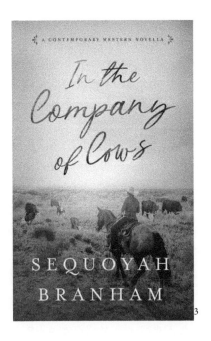[3]

No one listens to Nora Kelly, except her cows. Thanks to a lengthy drought, she is in danger of losing them, her livelihood, her job, and the one place she feels that she can truly be herself— the ranch.

The heifers never belittle or run her over when she tries to speak. They don't mind that she fumbles over her words– in fact, they are the only creatures who have ever just listened to her.

---

2. https://books2read.com/u/3Lx0AM

3. https://books2read.com/u/3Lx0AM

Unfortunately, no rain means no grass, and no grass means no cows. Nora's one hope is that her boss will find a new piece of land to lease, but they only have six weeks to secure a place and relocate. Determined to stay with the heifers, Nora scrounges up every ounce of bravery she has and goes to the only person who could possibly help: her intimidatingly successful uncle that she barely knows. He's a ranch real estate agent with connections, who doesn't have time for an awkward niece.

Just when a lease finally fits all of her boss' specifications, Nora discovers the land is already leased to her uncle, who might just be more family than she's ever experienced. What if her boss taking this lease breaks the budding bond between Nora and her uncle? But is she really willing to lose the only place she feels safe?

In the end, Nora must decide what staying in the company of cows is worth.

About the Author

Sequoyah Branham is passionate about sharing the beauty and heartbreak of ranching. Working on ranches across Texas gives her a wide variety of experiences to draw inspiration from for her characters and the obstacles they face. She enjoys long days in the saddle with good friends and her dog by her side as often as she can.

Catch up with her on her website www.sequoyahbranham.co

Milton Keynes UK
Ingram Content Group UK Ltd.
UKHW040254181024
449757UK00001B/15